She had too many responsibilities to have time to be interested in any man.

She saw the screen saver picture had come up—
a picture of Trent Dixon, a longtime friend and
coworker. Trent was carrying her son on his big
shoulders. Both guys were smiling as if they'd had
the time of their lives—and she suspected they had.

Katie quickly pushed a key and sent the image away
before melancholy could take hold. She'd made her
choices—and a relationship with Trent wasn't one
of them. She needed the brawny KCPD detective as
a friend—Tyler needed him as a friend—more than
she needed Trent to be a boyfriend or lover or even
something more.

Even if every cell in her body screamed to allow this
man into her heart.

KANSAS CITY CONFESSIONS

USA TODAY Bestselling Author

JULIE MILLER

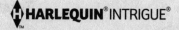

For my dear friend and fellow author Laura Landon.

She's a sweetie to travel to conferences with, and a tough ol' bird when it comes to motivating me. Love her!

Oh, and she writes wonderful historical romances, too.

ISBN-13: 978-0-373-69873-8

Kansas City Confessions

Copyright © 2015 by Julie Miller

Recycling programs for this product may not exist in your area.

Printed in U.S.A.

www.Harlequin.com

Julie Miller is an award-winning *USA TODAY* bestselling author of breathtaking romantic suspense—with a National Readers' Choice Award and a Daphne du Maurier Award among other prizes. She has also earned an *RT Book Reviews* Career Achievement Award. For a complete list of her books, monthly newsletter and more, go to juliemiller.org.

Books by Julie Miller

Harlequin Intrigue

The Precinct: Cold Case

The Precinct

The Precinct: Task Force

Visit the Author Profile page at Harlequin.com for more titles.

CAST OF CHARACTERS

Trent Dixon—KCPD detective who uses his brains as much as his considerable brawn to get information out of suspects. The one nut he can't crack? The girl he grew up across the street from—Katie Rinaldi. But everything changes when Katie and her son are threatened. Trent intends to keep this vulnerable family safe—and claim them for his own.

Katie Rinaldi—Her violent and troubled past makes this single mom particularly cautious about putting her trust in any man—even longtime friend Trent Dixon. As the Cold Case Squad's information technologist and resident computer genius, Katie is a walking encyclopedia of facts. Has her research into several unsolved murders put her on a killer's radar?

Tyler Rinaldi—Katie's son is playing Tiny Tim in a community theater production. His letter to Santa reveals that he's growing up way too fast. But his instincts to protect his mother may put him in harm's way.

Doug Price—Director of the community theater group putting on a production of Charles Dickens's *A Christmas Carol*.

Francis Sergel—Is this temperamental actor as creepy as the part he plays?

Leland Asher—The mob boss may be dying. But the smooth-talking criminal mastermind has a few loose ends to tie up before he goes.

Matt Asher—Leland's nephew. Is he his uncle's loyal right-hand man? Or is he setting up the ultimate betrayal?

Dr. Beverly Eisenbach—Leland's lady friend has visited him faithfully.

Craig Fairfax—The man who kidnapped Katie years earlier shared a cell block with Leland Asher. He knows what frightens her most.

The Host—Who is the architect behind several seemingly unsolvable murders?

Chapter One

"'God bless us, every one.'"

Katie Rinaldi joined the smattering of applause from the mostly empty seats of the Williams College auditorium, where the community theater group she belonged to was rehearsing a production of Charles Dickens's *A Christmas Carol*. The man with the white hair playing Ebenezer Scrooge stood at center stage, accepting handshakes and congratulations from the other actors as they completed their first technical rehearsal with sound and lights. The costumes she'd constructed for the three spirits seemed to be fitting just fine. And once she finished painting the mask for the Spirit of Christmas Future, she could sit back and enjoy the run of the show as an audience member. Okay, as a proud mama. She only had eyes for Tiny Tim.

She gave a thumbs-up sign to her third-grade son and laughed when he had to fight with the long sleeves of his costume jacket to free his hands and return the gesture. His rolling-eyed expression of frustration softened her laugh into an understanding smile.

She mouthed, *Okay. I'll fix it.* Once he was certain she'd gotten the message, Tyler Rinaldi turned to chatter with the boy next to him, who played one of his older

Cratchit brothers. One of the girls joined the group, bringing over a prop toy, and instantly, they were involved in a challenge to see who could get the wooden ball on an attached string into the cup first.

Although extra demands with her job at KCPD and the normal bustle of the holidays meant Katie was already busy without having to work a play into her schedule, she was glad she'd brought Tyler to auditions. The only child of a single mother, Tyler often spent his evenings alone with her, reading books or playing video or computer games after he finished his homework. She was glad to see him having fun and making friends.

"Note to self." Katie pulled her laptop from her lime-green-and-blue-flowered bag and opened up her calendar to type in a reminder that she needed to adjust the costume that had initially been made for a larger child. What was one less hour of sleep, anyway? "Shorten sleeves."

"I think we might just have a show." Katie startled at the hand on her shoulder. "Sorry. I didn't realize you were working."

Katie saved her calendar and turned in her seat to acknowledge the slender man with thick blond hair streaked with threads of gray sinking into the cushioned seat behind her. "Hey, Doug. I was just making some costume notes."

The play's director leaned forward, resting his arms on the back of the seat beside her. "You've done a nice job," he complimented, even though she'd been only one of several volunteers. His professionally trained voice articulated every word to dramatic perfection. "We're down to the details now—if the gremlins in this old theater will give us a break."

"Gremlins?"

Doug looked up into the steel rafters of the catwalk two stories above their heads before bringing his dark eyes back to hers. "I don't know a theater that isn't haunted. Or a production that feels like it's going to be ready in time. Those were brand-new battery packs we put in the microphones tonight, but they still weren't working."

"And you think the gremlins are responsible?" she teased.

Laughing, he patted her shoulder again. "More likely a short in a wire somewhere. But we need to figure out that glitch, put the finishing touches on makeup and costumes, and get the rest of the set painted before we open next weekend."

"You don't ask for much, do you?" she answered, subtly pulling away from his touch. Doug Price was one of those ageless-looking souls who could be forty or fifty or maybe even sixty but who had the energy—and apparently the libido—of a much younger man. "It's a fun holiday tradition that your group puts on this show every year. Tyler's having a blast being a part of it."

"And you?"

Katie smiled. Despite dodging a few touches and missing those extra hours of sleep, she'd enjoyed the creative energy she'd been a part of these past few weeks. "Me, too."

"Douglas?" A man's voice from the stage interrupted the conversation. Francis Sergel, the tall, gaunt gentleman who played the Spirit of Christmas Future, had a sharp, nasal voice. Fortunately, he'd gotten the role because he looked the part and didn't have to speak onstage. "Curtain calls? You said you'd block them this evening."

"In a minute." Doug's hand was on her shoulder again. "You want to go grab a coffee after rehearsal? My treat."

Although she knew him to be divorced, Doug was probably old enough to be her father, and she simply wasn't interested in his flirtations. She had too many responsibilities to have time to be interested in any man besides her son.

"Sorry. I've got work to finish." She gestured to her laptop and saw the screen-saver picture had come up—a picture of Trent Dixon, a longtime friend and coworker. Trent, a former college football player, was carrying her son on his big shoulders after a fun day spent in Columbia, Missouri, at a Mizzou football game. Dressed in black-and-gold jerseys and jeans, both guys were smiling as if they'd had the time of their lives—and she suspected they had. Trent was as good to Tyler now as he'd been to her back in high school when she'd been a brand-new teenage mom and she'd needed a real friend. As always, the image of man and boy made her smile…and triggered a little pang of regret.

Katie quickly pushed a key and sent the image away before that useless melancholy could take hold. She'd made her choices—and a relationship with Trent wasn't one of them. She needed the brawny KCPD detective as a friend—Tyler needed him as a friend—more than she needed Trent to be a boyfriend or lover or even something more. She'd nearly ruined that friendship back in high school. She'd nearly ruined her entire life with the foolish impulses she'd succumbed to back then. She wasn't going to make those mistakes again.

Katie pointed to the small brown-haired boy onstage. All her choices as an adult were based on whatever was best for her son. "It's a school night for Tyler, too. So we need to head home."

But Doug had seen the momentary trip down memory

lane in her lengthy pause. He reached over the seat to tap the edge of the laptop. "Was that Tyler's dad?"

The scent of gel or spray on his perfectly coiffed hair was a little overpowering as he brushed up beside her. Katie leaned to the far side of her seat to get some fresh air. "No. His father signed away his rights before Tyler was born. He's not in the picture."

She realized the tactical error as soon as the words left her mouth. Doug's grin widened as if she'd just given him a green light to hit on her. She mentally scrambled to backtrack and flashed a red light instead.

Easy. She clicked the mouse pad and pulled up the screen saver again, letting Trent's defensive-lineman shoulders and six feet five inches of height do their intimidation thing, even from a picture on a small screen. "This is Trent Dixon. He's a friend. A good friend," she emphasized, hoping Doug would interpret her longtime acquaintance with the boy who'd grown up across the street from her as a message that she wasn't interested in returning his nightly flirtations. "He's a cop. A KCPD detective."

If Trent's imposing size wasn't intimidating enough, the gun and badge usually ensured just about anybody's cooperation.

"I see. Maybe another time." Doug was king of his own little company of community theater volunteers and apparently didn't accept the word *no* from one of his lowly subjects. "I'll at least see you at the cast party after opening night, right?"

For Tyler's sake, she'd go and help her son celebrate his success—not because Doug kept asking her out. Katie lowered her head, brushing her thumb across the bottom of her keyboard, studying Trent's image as plan B popped into her head. Trent was Tyler's big buddy—the main male role model in her son's life besides her uncle Dwight, who'd taken her in when he'd married Katie's aunt Maddie nine years ago. Trent would be at the show's opening night. She'd make sure to introduce the big guy to Doug and let the handsy director rethink his efforts to date her. Katie was smiling at her evil little plan when she looked up again. "Sure. All three of us will be there."

"Doug?" Francis Sergel's voice had risen to a whiny pitch. "Curtain call?"

"I'm coming." The director waved off the middle-aged man with the beady dark eyes. "By the way, Tyler's done a great job memorizing his lines—faster than the other kids, and he's the youngest one."

Katie recognized the flattery for what it was, another attempt to make a connection with her. But she couldn't deny how proud she was of how her nine-year-old had taken to acting the way she once had. "Thanks. He's worked really hard."

"I can tell you've worked hard with him. He stays in character well, too."

"Douglas. Tonight?" Francis pulled the black hood off his head, although his dark, bushy beard and mustache still concealed half his face. "I'd like to get out of this costume."

"Coming." Doug squeezed her shoulder again as he stood. "See you tomorrow night." He clapped his hands to get everyone's attention onstage and sidled out into the aisle. "All right, cast—I need everybody's eyes right here."

But Francis's dark gaze held hers long enough to make her twitch uncomfortably in her seat. The man didn't need the Grim Reaper mask she was making for him. With his skin pinched over his bony cheeks and his eyes refusing to blink, he already gave her the willies. When he finally looked away and joined the clump of actors gathering center stage, Katie released the breath she hadn't known she'd been holding. What was that about?

Dismissing the man's interest as some kind of censure for keeping the director from doing his job, Katie turned to Tyler and winked. She tilted her head to encourage him to pay attention to Doug before she dropped her focus back to the computer in her lap. Francis was a bit of a diva on the best of nights. If he had a problem with Doug trying to make time with her, she'd send the actor straight to the source of the problem—aka, not her.

Feeling the need to tune out Doug and Francis and the prospect of another late night, Katie turned back to her computer. Blocking the final bows and running them a few times would take several minutes, leaving her the opportunity to get a little work done and hopefully free up some time once she got home and put Tyler to bed.

With quick precision, she keyed in the password to access encrypted work files she'd been organizing for the police department—sometimes on the clock, sometimes in her own spare time. Katie had spent months scanning in unsolved case files and loading the data into the cross-referencing computer program she'd designed. Okay, so maybe her work as an information specialist with KCPD's cold case squad wasn't as exciting as the acting career she'd dreamed of before a teenage pregnancy and harrowing kidnapping plot to sell her unborn son in a black-market baby ring had altered her life plan. But it was a good, steady paycheck that allowed her to support herself and Tyler single-handedly.

Besides, the technical aspects of her work had never stopped Katie from thinking, imagining, creating. She loved the challenge of fitting together the pieces of a puzzle on an old unsolved case—not to mention the satisfaction of knowing she was doing something meaningful with her life. She hadn't had the best start in the world—her abusive father had murdered her mother and been sent to prison. Helping the police catch bad guys went a long way toward redeeming herself for some of the foolish mistakes she'd made as an impulsive, grieving young woman trying to atone for her father's terror. Working with computers and data was a job her beloved aunt Maddie and uncle Dwight, Kansas City's district attorney, understood and respected. She would always be grateful to the two of them for rescuing her and Tyler and giving her a real home. Although she knew they would support her even if she had chosen to become an actress, this career choice was one way she could honor and thank them for taking her in and loving her like a daughter. Plus, even though he didn't quite grasp the research and technical details of her job, Tyler thought her work was pretty cool. Hanging out with all those cops and helping them solve crimes put her on a tiny corner of the shelf beside his comic book and cartoon action heroes. Making her son proud was a gift she wouldn't trade for any spotlight.

Katie sorted through the first file that came up, highlighting words such as the victim's name, witnesses who'd been interviewed, suspect lists and evidence documentation and dropping them into the program that would match up any similarities between this unsolved murder and other crimes in the KCPD database. The tragic death of a homeless man back in the '70s had few clues and fewer suspects, sadly, making it a quick case to read through and document. Others often took hours, or even days, to sort and categorize. But she figured LeRoy Byrd had been important to someone, and therefore, it was important to her to get his information out of a musty storage box and transferred into the database.

"There you go, LeRoy." She patted his name on the screen. "It's not much. Just know we're still thinking about you and working on your case."

She closed out his information and pulled up the next file, marked *Gemma Gordon*. Katie's breath shuddered in her chest as she looked into the eyes of a teenage girl who'd been missing for ten years. "Not you, too."

The temperature in the auditorium seemed to drop a good twenty degrees as memories of her own kidnapping nightmare surfaced. This girl was seventeen, the same age Katie had been when she'd gone off to find her missing friend, Whitney. Katie had found her friend, all right, but had become a prisoner herself, kept alive until she could give birth to Tyler and her kidnappers tried to sell him in a black-market adoption scheme. Thanks to her aunt and uncle, Tyler was saved and Katie had escaped with her life. But Whitney hadn't been so lucky.

She touched her fingers to the young girl's image on the screen and skimmed through her file. The similarities between the old Katie and this girl were frightening. Pregnant. Listed as a runaway. Katie had fought to save her child. Had Gemma Gordon? Had she even had a chance to fight? Katie had found a family with her aunt Maddie and uncle Dwight and survived. Was anyone missing this poor girl? According to the file, neither Gemma Gordon nor her baby had ever been found.

"You must have been terrified," Katie whispered, feeling the grit of tears clogging her throat. She read on through the persons of interest interviewed in the initial investigation. "What...?" She swiped away the moisture that had spilled onto her cheek and read the list again. There was one similarity too many to her own nightmare—a name she'd hoped never to see again. "No. No, no."

Katie's fingers hovered above the keyboard. One click. A few seconds of unscrambling passwords and a lie about her clearance level and she could find out everything she wanted to about the name on the screen. She could find out what cell he was in at the state penitentiary, who his visitors were, if his name had turned up in conjunction with any other kidnappings or missing-person cases. With a few keystrokes she could know if the man with that name was enjoying a healthy existence or rotting away in prison the way she'd so often wished over the years.

When a hot tear plopped onto the back of her knuckles, Katie startled. She willed herself out of the past and dabbed at her damp cheeks with the sleeve of her sweater. Beyond the fact that hacking into computer systems she didn't officially have access to without a warrant could get her fired, she knew better than to give in to the fears and anger and grief. Katie straightened in her seat and quickly highlighted the list of names, entering them all into the database. "You're a survivor, Katie Lee Rinaldi. Those people can't hurt you anymore. You beat them."

But Gemma Gordon hadn't.

After swiping away another tear, Katie sent the list into the database before logging out. She turned off the portable Wi-Fi security device on the seat beside her and shut down her laptop. She squeezed the edge of her computer as if she was squeezing that missing girl's hand. "I'll do whatever I can to help you, too, Gemma. I promise."

When she looked up, she realized she was the only

parent left in the auditorium seats. The stage was empty, too. "Oh, man."

How long had she been sitting there, caught up in the past? Too long. Her few minutes of work had stretched on longer than she'd thought, and the present was calling. She stuffed her equipment back into her flowered bag and stood, grabbing her wool coat off the back of her seat and pulling it on. "Tyler?"

Katie looped her bag over her shoulder and scooted toward the end of the row of faded green folding seats. As pretentious and egotistical as Doug Price could be, he also ran a tight ship. Since they were borrowing this facility from the college, there were certain rules he insisted they all follow. Props returned to backstage tables. Costumes on hangers in the dressing rooms. Rehearsal started when he said it would and ended with the same punctuality. Campus security checked the locks at ten thirty, so every night they were done by ten.

Katie pulled her cell phone from her bag and checked the time when she reached the sloping aisle—ten fifteen. She groaned. The cast was probably backstage, changing into their street clothes if they hadn't already left, and Doug was most likely up in the tech booth, giving the sound and light guys their notes.

Exchanging her phone for the mittens in her pocket, Katie hurried down the aisle toward the stage. "Tyler? Sorry I got distracted. You ready to go, bud?"

And that was when the lights went out.

Chapter Two

"Ow." Disoriented by the sudden darkness, Katie bumped into the corner of a seat. Leaning into the most solid thing she could find, she grabbed the back of the chair and held on while she got her bearings. "Hey! I'm still in the house."

Her voice sounded small and muffled in the cavernous space as she waited several seconds for a response. But the only answer was the scuffle of hurried footsteps moving over the carpet at the very back of the auditorium.

She spun toward the sound. "Hello?" She squeezed her eyes shut against the dizziness that pinballed through her brain. Only her grip on the chair kept her on her feet while her equilibrium righted itself. She heard a loud clank and the protesting squeak of the old hinges as whoever was in here with her scooted out the door to the lobby. Opening her eyes, Katie lifted her blind focus up the sloping aisle. "Tyler? This isn't a good time to play hide-and-seek."

Why weren't the security lights coming on? They ran on a separate power source from the rest of the theater. "Did we have a power outage?"

Why wouldn't anybody answer her? Panic tried to lock up the air in her chest. The dark wasn't a safe place to be. She'd been reading those old case files, had lingered over the pregnant teen whose kidnapping and unsolved murder would have been Katie's story if she hadn't been lucky—if her aunt and uncle hadn't moved heaven and earth to find her. Why did it have to be so dark? Maybe that had been Doug or the security guard or some other Good Samaritan rushing out to get upstairs to the tech booth in the balcony. She just needed to be patient.

Only it felt as though several minutes had passed, and the lights still weren't coming on. Maybe it had only been seconds. But even seconds were too long in a blackout like this. She swayed against the remembered images of hands grabbing her in the night, of her dead friend Whitney and a teenage girl whose life and death had been relegated to a dusty cold case file.

"Stop it." Rubbing at the bruise forming on her hip, letting the soreness clear her mind, Katie forced her eyes open, willing her vision to focus in the darkness and her memories to blur. Her work took her to the past, but she lived in the here and now. With Tyler. He'd be frightened of the pitch-black, too. She had to find her son. "Think, woman," she challenged herself. "Tyler?"

But the only change in the shroud of blackness was her brain finally kicking into gear.

"Ugh. You're an idiot." Rational thought finally returned and she pulled out her phone, adjusting the screen to flashlight mode to make sure someone could see her before shining it up toward the tech booth in the balcony and shouting again. "Lights, please? Doug?" Her light wasn't that powerful, but the booth looked dark, too. "Is anybody up there? I'm on my way out. My son's here, too. Please."

She waited in silence for several more seconds before she heard a soft click from the stage. She turned and saw the ropes of running lights that marked the edge and wings of the performance space had come on. *This way*, they beckoned. Really? That was the help she was going to get? Put in place to help the actors find their way off-stage during a blackout at the end of a scene, the small red bulbs barely created a glow in the shadows.

"Thanks! For nothing," she added under her breath, pointing her phone light to the floor to illuminate the stairs she climbed to get onto the stage. Somebody with a twisted sense of humor must be trying to teach her a lesson about her tardiness. Up here, at least, she could follow the dimly lit path the actors did, and she ended up pushing through the side curtains to get to the backstage doors and greenroom and dressing areas beyond.

Her stomach twisted into a knot when she pushed open the heavy firewall door. It was dark back here, too. Her annoyance with Doug turned to trepidation in a heartbeat. "This isn't funny," she called out. Where had everybody gone? Where was her son? "Tyler? Sweetie, answer me."

She kicked the doorstop to the floor to prop the steel door open. Okay. If somebody wanted to spook her, wanted to teach her a lesson about keeping others late at the theater, he or she had succeeded.

But with her son missing, she couldn't allow either fear or anger to take hold. Katie breathed in deeply, waiting until she could hear the silence over the thumping of her heart before following her light into the greenroom, or cast waiting area. Turning her phone to the wall, she found the light switch and lifted it. Nothing.

Had someone forgotten to pay the light bill? Was the college saving money by turning off the electricity after ten? She glanced back toward the stage. The running lights were still glowing. Even if they were battery-powered, someone had to have turned them on. And she knew she hadn't imagined those footsteps earlier. She wasn't alone.

"Tyler, honey, if you're playing some kind of game, this isn't funny." She shouted for the security guard who worked in the building most nights. "Mr. Thompson?"

Was Doug Price playing a trick on her for turning him down again? Did he think she'd be freaked out enough that she'd run to him and expect him to be her hero? If that was what this was about… Her blood heated, chasing away the worried chill. Oh, she was so never going out with that guy. "Tyler? Where are you?"

Why didn't he answer? Had he fallen asleep? Had something happened to him?

Uh-uh. She wasn't going there.

Katie shined her light into the men's dressing room. Lights off. Room empty. She sorted through the costumes hanging on the rack there, peeked beneath the counter. Nothing. She opened the door to the ladies' dressing room, too, and repeated the search.

"Tyler Rinaldi, you answer—"

A boot dropped to the floor behind the rack of long dresses and ghostly costumes. Katie cried out as the layers of polyester, petticoats, wool and lace toppled over on top of her. Hands pushed through the cascade of clothes, knocking her down with them. "Hey! What are you…? Help! Stop!"

She hit the tile floor on her elbows and bottom, and the impact tingled through her fingers, jarring loose her grip on the phone. Her assailant was little more than a wisp of shadow in the dark room. But there was no mistaking the slamming door or the drumbeat of footsteps running across the concrete floor of the work space and storage area behind the stage.

Katie's thoughts raced as she clawed her way free through the pile of fallen clothes and felt around in the darkness to retrieve her phone. Had she interrupted a robbery? There were power tools for set construction and sound equipment and some antiques they were using as props. All those things should be locked up, but an outsider might not know that. Was this some kind of college prank by a theater student? Could it be something personal? She wouldn't have expected Doug to get physical like that. Had she offended someone else?

Her fingers brushed across the protective plastic case of her phone and she snatched it up. She pushed to her feet and smacked into the closed door. "Let me out!" She slapped at the door with her palm until she found the door handle and pulled it open. "Stay away from my son! Tyler!"

But by the time she ran out into the backstage area in pursuit of the shadow, the footsteps had gone silent. The exit door on the far side of the backstage area stood wide open and a slice of light from the sidewalk lamp outside cut clear across the room. After so long in the darkness with just the illumination from her phone, Katie had to avert her eyes from even that dim glow. She saw nothing more than a wraithlike glimpse of a man slipping through the doorway into the winter night outside.

Following the narrowing strip of light, she stumbled forward, dodging prop tables and flats until the door closed with a quiet click and she was plunged into another blackout.

She stopped in her tracks. The one thing she hated more than the darkness was not knowing if her son was safe. And since she couldn't find him...

She pushed a command on her phone and raised it to her lips. "Call Trent."

Inching forward without any kind of light now, she counted off each ring of the telephone as she waited for her strong, armed, utterly reliable friend to pick up. She thought she could make out the red letters of the exit sign above the door by the time Trent cut off the fourth ring and picked up.

"Hey, sunshine," he greeted on a breathless gasp of air. "It's a little late. What's up?"

Oblivious to the current irony of his nickname for her, Katie squeezed her words past the panic choking her throat. "I'm at the theater… The lights…" She bumped into the edge of a flat and shifted course. "Ow. Damn it. I can't see…"

A warm chuckle colored the detective's audible breathing. "Did you leave your car lights on again? Need me to come jump-start it?"

"No." Well, technically, she didn't know that, but she didn't think she had.

"Flat tire? Williams College is a good twenty minutes from here, but I could—"

"Trent. Listen to me. There is some kind of weird…" As his deep inhales and exhales calmed, she heard a tuneless kind of percussive music and a woman's voice laughing in the background. *The man is breathless from exertion, Katie. Get a clue.* "Oh, God," she mumbled as realization dawned and embarrassment warmed her skin. "I'm so sorry. Is someone with you?"

Instead of answering her question, Trent's tone changed from winded amusement to that steely deep tone that resonated through his chest and reminded her he was a cop. "Weird? How? Are you all right? Is Tyler okay?"

Trent Dixon was on a date. He might be in the middle of *more* than a date. She'd forgotten about setting him up with that friend from the coffee shop a few weeks back. Trent wasn't her knight in shining armor to call whenever she had a problem she couldn't fix. He wasn't Tyler's father and he wasn't her boyfriend. Trent was just the good guy who'd grown up across the street and had a hard time saying no to her. Knowing that about him, because she was his friend, too, she'd worked really hard not to take advantage of his good-guy tendencies and protective instincts. "Is that Erin Ballard? I'm sorry. I wasn't thinking. You have company."

"I dropped Erin off an hour ago after dinner. I stopped by the twenty-four-hour gym because I needed to work off some excess energy. And it's too cold to go for a run outside." He paused for a moment, wiping down with a towel or catching his breath. "Apparently, I'm not the only night-owl fitness freak in KC."

He felt energized after his date with Erin? Was that *excess energy* a code for sexual frustration? Had he wanted something more from Erin besides dinner and conversation? Or had he gotten exactly what he wanted and was now on some kind of endorphin high that wouldn't let him sleep? The momentary stab of jealousy at the thought of Trent bedding the willowy blonde she'd introduced him to ended as she tripped over the leg of a chair in the darkness. "Damn it."

"Katie?"

"I'm sorry." She should be thinking of her son, not Trent. Not any misplaced feelings of envy for the woman who landed him. Tyler was the only person who mattered right now. And a panicked late-night call to a man she had no claim on wasn't going to help. "Never mind. I'm sorry to interrupt your evening. It's late and I need to get Tyler home to bed. Tell Erin hi for me."

"Katie Lee Rinaldi," Trent chided. "Why did you call me?"

"I'll handle it myself."

"Handle what? Damn it, woman, talk to me."

"Sorry. I don't need you to rescue me every time I make a mistake. Enjoy your date."

"I'm not on a… Katie?"

"Good night." She disconnected the call, ending the interrogation.

Seconds later, the phone vibrated in her hand. The big galoot. He'd called her right back. Not only did she feel guilty for interrupting his evening, but now she realized just how crazy she'd sounded. Practically perfect Erin Ballard would never panic like this and make a knee-jerk call to a friend for help.

Pull it together and think rationally. She should simply call 9-1-1 and report a break-in or say that an intruder had vandalized the lights in the theater. She could call Uncle Dwight. But as Kansas City's DA, it would only be a matter of minutes before half the police department knew that she'd lost her son and wasn't fit to be his mother.

Katie inhaled a deep breath, pushing aside that option as a last resort. She didn't ever want to be labeled that impulsive, needs-to-be-rescued woman she'd been as a teenager again. Katie Rinaldi stood on her own two feet. She took care of her own son. The two of them would never end up like the girl in that file again.

"Tyler!" With her phone on flashlight mode once more, she hurried as quickly as she dared toward the exit sign. "If you are playing some kind of game with me, mister, I'm grounding you until you're eighteen."

Silence was her only answer.

Had Tyler gotten tired of waiting for his flaky, work-obsessed mother and headed on out to the car? Or was he still inside someplace, trapped in the darkness like she was? Why didn't he answer? *Could* he answer?

First that damn case file and now this? She couldn't stop the nightmarish memory this time. Her feet turned to lead. Katie didn't have to close her eyes to remember the hand over her mouth. The prick of a needle in her arm. Her limbs going numb. Cradling her swollen belly and crying out for her baby as she collapsed into a senseless heap. The night she'd been abducted she'd gone to help Whitney and wound up in the same mess herself. A few weeks later, she'd given birth to Tyler in a sterile room with no one to hold her hand or urge her to breathe, and she'd nearly given up all hope of surviving.

But the tiny little boy the kidnappers laid in her arms for a few seconds had changed everything, giving her a reason to survive, a reason to escape, a reason to keep fighting.

If anything happened to her son…

If he'd been taken from her again…

Finally. Her palm flattened against ice-cold steel. Burying her fears and summoning her maternal strength, Katie shoved open the back door. A blast of bitter cold and snowy crystals melting against her nose and cheeks cleared her thoughts. "Tyler!"

It was brighter outside the theater, even though it was night. The campus lights were on, and each lamppost was adorned with shiny silver wreaths that shimmered with the cold, damp wind. The rows of lights illuminated the path down into the woods behind the auditorium and marked the sidewalk that led around the back of the theater to the parking lot on the north side. New snow was falling, capturing the light from the lamps and reflecting their orange glow into the air around her.

There were dozens of footprints in the first layer of snow from where the cast and crew had exited out to their cars. But there was one set of man-size prints leading down the walkway into the trees, disappearing at the footbridge that arched over the creek at the bottom of the hill. Good. Run. Whoever had been in the darkened building with her was gone.

But the freezing air seeped right into her bones when she read the hastily carved message in the snow beside the tracks.

Stop before someone gets hurt.

She shivered inside her coat. "Gets hurt?" She looked out into the woods, wondering if the man who'd trapped her in the dressing room was still here, watching. "Stop what? What do you want? Tyler?"

Confusion gave way to stark, cold fear when she zeroed in on the impression of a small, size-five tennis shoe, left by a brown-haired boy who hated to wear his winter boots. She hoped. The prints followed the same path as the senseless message. "Tyler!"

Thinking more than panicking now, Katie searched the shadows near the door until she found a broom beside the trash cans there. She wedged the broom handle between the door and frame in case the footprints were a false hope and she needed to get back inside the theater and search some more. She followed the smaller track down the hill. Had the man taken her son? Convinced him to come along with him to find his missing mother? Had she been stuck inside the building for that long?

But suddenly, the boy-size footprints veered off into

the trees. Katie stepped knee-deep into the drift next to the sidewalk, ignored the snow melting into her jeans and headed into the woods. "Tyler!"

She heard a dog barking from somewhere in the distance. Oh, no. There was one thing she knew could make her son forget every bit of common sense she'd taught him. The boy-size prints were soon joined by a set of paw prints half the size of her fist. Both tracks ran back up the hill toward the parking lot, and Katie followed. "Please be chasing that stupid dog. Please don't let anyone have taken my son. Tyler!"

The trail led her back to the sidewalk and disappeared around the corner of the building. Katie broke into a run once she cleared the snow among the trees and followed the tracks into the open expanse of asphalt and snow. She was almost light-headed with relief when she spotted the boy in the dark blue parka, playing with a skinny, short-haired collie mix in the parking lot. "Tyler!"

A blur of tan and white dashed off into the woods, followed by clouds of hot, steamy dog breath and a boy's dejected sigh.

Thank God. Tyler was safe.

Sparing one moment of concern for the familiar collarless stray disappearing into the snowy night, Katie ran straight to her son and pulled him into her chest for a tight hug. She kissed the top of his wool stocking cap, hugged him tighter and kissed him again. "Oh, thank goodness. Thank goodness, sweetie."

"Mo-om," Tyler whined on two different pitches before pushing enough space between them for him to tilt his face up to hers. "You scared him away."

Katie eased her grip around her son's slim shoulders and brought her mittened hands up to cup his freckled cheeks and look down into those bright blue eyes that matched her own. "I was so scared. There was a blackout inside the theater and I couldn't find you." Since running across the parking lot in panic mode and hugging the stuffing out of him had probably already worried him enough, Katie opted to leave out any mention of the cryptic message in the snow or the man who'd pushed her down in the dressing room. "I kept calling for you, but you didn't answer. What are you doing out here?"

"Feeding Padre. Doug told me he was out here again tonight, so I came to see him."

"Doug did?" Why would the director send her child out of the theater on such a bitter night?

"He said he'd tell you where I was." But Doug hadn't. "I think Padre's hungry, so I saved my peanut butter sandwich from lunch for him."

Still feeling uneasy, her breath came in ragged puffs while Tyler knelt down to stuff an empty plastic bag into the book bag at his feet. Katie looked all around the well-lit but empty lot to verify that her red Kia was the only vehicle there and that no one else was loitering about. If Doug had meant to tell her Tyler's whereabouts, he'd forgotten amid the busyness of shutting down a tech rehearsal and had apparently gone home without giving her mother's concern a second thought. Maybe the mixup was all perfectly innocent. But if he'd done it on purpose...

"Come on, sweetie. We need to go." Katie draped her arm around Tyler's shoulders when he stood back up and hurried him along beside her to the car. "Didn't you eat your lunch?"

"Most of it. But I can always have a bowl of cereal

when we get home, and Padre doesn't have anybody to feed him."

"Padre?" She swapped her phone for the keys in her coat pocket and unlocked the car.

Tyler opened the passenger door and climbed inside on his knees, tossing his book bag into the backseat. "Did you see the ring of white fur around his neck? It looks like the collar Pastor Bill wears, and everybody calls him Padre."

Katie closed the door and hurried around the front of the car to get in behind the wheel. Naming a dog she knew he couldn't have was probably a bad thing, but she was more worried about blackouts and intruders and not being able to find her son. She placed her bag in the backseat beside Tyler's, locked the doors and quickly started the engine so she could crank up the heat. "Why didn't you wait for me? Or come get me as soon as you'd changed? I'm sorry I got distracted, but I was sitting out in the au- ditorium. I would have come to feed the dog with you. You shouldn't be out here by yourself, especially at night."

Tyler turned around and plopped down into his seat. "I know. But I wanted to see Padre before one of the other kids got to him first. He likes me, Mom. He lets me pet him and doesn't bite me or anything. Wyatt already has a dog, and Kayla's family has two cats. So he should be mine."

She grimaced at the sad envy for two of the other chil- dren in the play. "Tyler—"

"When everybody else started to leave, I tried to get back in, but the door was locked. So I stayed outside to play with Padre."

"Is that the real story? I don't mean the dog. Doug sending you outside? Getting locked out?" She pulled off her mitten and reached across the car to cup his cheek.

Chilled, but healthy. She was the only one having heart palpitations tonight. "There wasn't anyone left in the cast or crew to let you back in?"

"Maybe if I had my own cell phone, I could have called you."

"Really?" She pushed his stocking cap up to the crown of his head and ruffled his wavy dark hair between her fingers. "I was scared to death that something had happened to you, and you're playing that card?"

He fastened his seat belt. "I put a phone on my Christmas list."

"We talked about this. Not until middle school."

"Johnny Griffith has one."

"I'm not Johnny Griffith's mom." Katie straightened in her seat to fasten her own seat belt. "You're up past your bedtime. Let's go home before your toes freeze."

"Did Doug ask you out again?" Tyler asked. "Is that why he wanted to get rid of me?"

She glanced over at the far too wise expression on her son's freckled face. "He did. I told him no again, too."

Tyler tugged off his mittens and held his pink fingers up in front of the heating vent. "I thought maybe you were still in there talking to him. He's a good director and all, but I don't want him to be my dad."

Katie reached for Tyler's hands and pulled them between hers to rub some love and warmth into them. "He won't be." Not that he'd had a chance, anyway. But endangering her son certainly checked him off the list. "I can guarantee that."

"Good." When he'd had enough of a warming reassurance, Tyler pulled away and kicked his feet together, knocking snow off his shoes onto the floor mat. "Do you think Padre's toes will freeze out there tonight? Dogs have toes, right?"

"They do. But he must have dug himself a snow cave or found someplace warm to sleep if he's survived a whole week outdoors in the wintertime. I think he'll be okay. I hope he will be." Katie smiled wryly before turning on the windshield wipers and clearing away the wet snow. She shifted the car into gear, but paused with her foot on the brake to inspect the empty parking lot one more time. Maybe Tyler hadn't been in any danger. Maybe she hadn't really been, either. But why leave that message? And if the intruder had run along the pathway, had Tyler seen him either sneak into the building or run out of it? The man could easily have parked in another area of the campus so she wouldn't be able to spot him. But could Tyler have gotten a description that might put him in some kind of future harm? Her grip tightened around the steering wheel. "Did anybody talk to you while you were out here by yourself?"

"Wyatt and Kayla said goodbye. Kayla's dad asked me if you were still here. I told him as long as the car was, you were, too."

She'd make a point to thank Mr. Hudnall for checking on her son tomorrow night. "I meant a stranger. Anybody you didn't know? Was anyone watching you or following you?"

Tyler dropped his head back in dramatic groan. "I know about stranger danger. I would have shouted really loud or run really fast or gotten into the car with Kayla's dad because I know him."

"Okay, sweetie. Just checking."

He sat up straight and turned in his seat. "But if I had a phone—"

"Maybe later." She laughed and lifted her foot off the brake. "I need to talk it over with Aunt Maddie and Uncle Dwight first. We're on their phone plan."

And now the sulky lip went out. "Am I going to get anything that's on my Christmas list?"

"There are already some presents under the tree."

"None of them are big enough to be a dog. And none of them are small enough to be a phone. They're probably socks and underwear."

"I'm sure you'd be really good with a pet, sweetie, but you know we can't have a dog in our apartment." She pulled the car up next to the sidewalk at the corner of the theater building. "Hold on a second. I propped the door open in case I couldn't find you out here. I need to go close it so we don't get in trouble with the college. Sit tight. Lock yourself in until I get back."

After pulling her lime-green mittens back on and tying her scarf more tightly around her neck, Katie climbed out, waited for Tyler to relock the doors and hurried back to the exit. She glanced through the woods and walkway for the stray dog or a more menacing figure, but saw no sign of movement among the trees and shadows. But she slowed her steps once she shifted her full attention to the door. It was already closed, sealed tight. Had she not wedged the broom in securely enough?

Pulling her phone from her pocket again, Katie checked the time before turning on the camera. She'd only been gone a few minutes, hardly enough time for the security guard to make his rounds. And if he'd been close by already, why wouldn't he have answered her shouts of distress or turned on a light for her to see?

Who had closed this door? The same unseen person

who'd flipped on the running lights and hidden in the dark theater?

The man who'd run off into the woods after knocking her off her feet?

No matter what the answers to any of those questions might be, Katie worked around enough cops to know that details mattered. So she moved past the door and angled her phone camera down to take a picture of the disturbing message.

Her breath rushed out in a warm white cloud in the air, and she couldn't seem to breathe in again.

The message was gone.

The marks of her heeled boots were clear in the new layer of snow. But the rest of the footprints—boy-size tennis shoes, paw prints, the long, wide imprints of a stranger running away from the theater—*Stop before someone gets hurt*—had all been swept away.

A chill skittered down the back of her neck. She was bundled up tight enough to know it wasn't the snow getting to her skin. This was wrong. This was intentional. This was personal.

Katie backed away from the door. The man inside the theater had come back. He could still be here—hiding in the trees, lurking on the other side of that door, watching her right now. Waiting for her.

She glanced back and forth, trying to see into the night beyond the lamplights and the snow. Nothing. No one. She hadn't seen the man who grabbed her the night she'd been kidnapped, either.

She was shaking now. Katie didn't feel safe.

Her son wasn't safe.

"Tyler." She whispered his name like a storm cloud in the air as she turned and raced back to the car, banging on the window until Tyler unlocked the door and she could slip inside. She relocked the doors and peeled off her mittens before reaching across the seat and cupping his cheek in her palm again. "I love you, sweetie."

His skin was toasty warm from the heater, but she was shivering inside her coat as she shifted into gear and sped across the parking lot to the nearest exit.

"Mom? What's wrong?"

Tyler's voice was frightened, unsure. She was supposed to be his rock. She was a horrible mother for worrying him with her paranoid imagination. She was putting him in danger by not thinking straight.

"I'm sorry, sweetie. I'm okay. We're both okay." She shook the snowflakes from her dark hair, smiled for him, then pulled out onto the street at a much safer speed. "Why don't you tell me more about Padre."

"CONFOUNDED WOMAN." Trent slowed his pickup to a crawl once he saw that the parking lot outside the Williams College auditorium had nothing but asphalt and snow to greet him after his zip across Kansas City to get to Katie and Tyler.

As he circled the perimeter of the empty lot, just to make sure he hadn't misunderstood the location of the distress call, and the tiny Rinaldi family truly wasn't stranded someplace out in the bitter cold, Trent admitted that Katie Lee Rinaldi knew how to push his buttons— even though she never did it intentionally. It was his own damn fault. If he hadn't felt especially protective of Katie ever since she'd decided back in high school he was the one friend she could rely on without question, and if all the hours he'd spent with Tyler didn't make him think he wanted to be a father more than just about anything—

more than making sergeant, more than playing for the Chiefs, more than wishing he didn't have the time bomb of one concussion too many ticking in his head—then he wouldn't charge off on these fool's errands to protect a family that wasn't his.

He pulled up at the sidewalk near the auditorium's back entrance and shifted the truck into Park. He'd left before finishing a perfectly good workout to find out what Katie's phone call had been about when he'd barely been able to work up a polite interest in lingering on Erin Ballard's door-step and trading a good-night kiss. Erin was an attractive blonde who could carry on an intelligent conversation, and who'd made it perfectly clear that she'd like Trent to come in out of the cold for some hot coffee and anything else he might want. Erin wasn't impulsive. Her wardrobe consisted of beiges and browns, and nothing she'd said or done had surprised him. Not once. Cryptic phone calls, leading with her heart and putting loyalty before common sense were probably foreign concepts. If it wasn't on Erin's planner in her phone, it probably wouldn't happen. Erin wasn't inter-esting to Trent.

She wasn't Katie.

No woman was.

The proof was in the follow-up buzz in his pocket. Trent checked his phone again, admitting he was less frustrated to read the Are you mad at me? text from Erin than he was to see that he hadn't heard boo from Katie since she'd called about witnessing something *weird* and had sounded so afraid.

No. Busy. With work, he added before sending the text to Erin. Maybe the woman would get a clue and stop pes-tering him. He'd already turned down her efforts to take a couple of dates to the next level as gently as he could, and he was done dealing with her tonight.

But he wasn't done with Katie.

After pulling his black knit watch cap down over his ears and putting his glove back on, Trent killed the engine and climbed out for a closer look. Because he was a cop and panicked phone calls about something *weird* happening at the theater tended to raise his suspicions, and because it was Katie, who was not only a friend since high school but also a coworker on the cold case squad, Trent wasn't about to ignore the call and drive home without at least verifying that whatever problem had prompted her call was no longer anything to worry about.

Not that he really knew what the problem was. Trent pulled a flashlight from the pocket of his coat and shined the light out into the foggy woods at the edge of the lot before clearing his head with a deep breath of the bracing air. The snow drifted against the brick wall of the building and crunched beneath his boots as he set out to walk the perimeter and do a little investigating before he followed up with Katie to find out what the hell she'd been babbling about.

Katie had been frightened—that much he could hear in her voice. But she'd never really answered any of his questions. He didn't know if she was having trouble with her car again, if something had happened to Tyler, if she was in some kind of danger or if she'd gone off to help a friend who needed something. With his interrogation skills, he could get straight answers from frightened witnesses with nervous gaps in their memories and lying lowlifes who typically avoided the truth as a means of survival.

But could he get a straight answer from Katie Rinaldi?

He checked the main entrance first but found all the

front doors locked. He identified himself with his badge and briefly chatted with the security guard, who reported that the campus had been quiet that evening, that the on-campus and commuter students alike had pretty much stayed either in the buildings or made a quick exit in their cars as soon as evening classes had ended. Nobody was hanging out any longer than necessary to tempt the weather or waste time in these last days before finals week and Christmas break. After thanking the older man and assuring him he was here on unofficial police business and that there was no need to call for backup or stop making his rounds, Trent followed the lit pathway around the rest of the building. Other than the campus officer's car, the staff lot to the south was empty, too.

Unwilling to write the call for help off just yet, Trent circled to the back of the auditorium. But when the chomp of snow beneath his steps fell silent, Trent looked down. "Interesting."

What kind of maintenance crew would take the time to clear a sidewalk at this time of night when the snow wasn't scheduled to stop falling for another couple hours? Trent knelt and plucked a bristle broken off a corn broom from the dusting of snow accumulating again beneath his feet. And what kind of professionals with an entire campus to clear would bother with a broom when they had snowblowers and even larger machinery at their disposal?

Had there been a prowler near the building who'd swept away any evidence of lurking on campus? Was that what Katie had called him about? Had she seen someone trying to break in? Had the perp seen her? With his hackles rising beneath the collar of his coat, Trent pushed to his feet, noting where the new snow had been swept away—around the locked back door and down the sidewalk into the trees. He'd qualify that as *weird*. The scenario fit some kind of cover-up.

"Katie?" There'd better not be an answer. He raised his voice, praying the woods were quiet because the Rinaldis were safely home, asleep in their beds. "Tyler?"

His nape itched with the sensation of being watched, and Trent casually turned his light down along the path between the trees. Was that a rustle of movement in the low brush? Or merely the wind stirring the branches of a pine tree? The lamps along the sidewalk created circles of light that made it impossible to see far into the woods. With his ears attuned to any unusual sound in the cold night air, he moved along the cleared walk down toward the frozen creek at the bottom of the hill. "KCPD! You in the trees, show yourself."

His deep voice filled the air without an answer.

"Katie?" His gloved fingers brushed against the phone in his pocket. Maybe he should just call her. But the hour was late and Tyler would be in bed and a phone ringing at this hour would probably cause more alarm than reassurance. Besides, if she wouldn't give him any kind of explanation when she called him, he doubted she'd be any more forthcoming when he called her. He'd give this search a few more minutes until he could say good-night to the suspicions that put him on guard and go home to get some decent shut-eye himself.

When he reached the little arched bridge that crossed the creek, *weird* took a disquieting turn into *what the hell?* Trent stopped in the middle of the bridge, looking down at both sides—the one that had been deliberately cleared from the back door of the theater down to this point, and the two inches of snow on the sidewalk beyond the creek marked by a clear set of tracks. There were two skid marks through the snow, as if someone had slipped on the bridge and fallen, then a trail of footsteps leading up the hill on the opposite side. One set of tracks. Man-size. More than that, the distance between the steps lengthened, as though whoever had left the trail had decided he needed to run. A man in a hurry—running from something or to something or because of something. A student in a hurry to get to his dorm or car? Or a man running away from campus security and a cop who might be curious about why he'd want to erase his trail?

Where had this guy gone, anyway? The snow was coming down heavily enough that those tracks should be nothing but a bunch of divots in the icy surface if they'd been there when classes had been dismissed or Tyler's rehearsal had ended. These were deep. These were recent. These were—

Trent spun when he heard the noise crashing through the drifts and underbrush toward him. He'd pulled up his coat and had his hand on the butt of his gun when a blur of tan and white shot out between the trees and darted around his legs. "What the...?"

Four legs. Black nose. Long tail.

After one more scan to make sure the dog was the only thing coming at him, Trent laughed and eased the insulated nylon back over his holster. "Hey, pup. See anybody but me out here tonight?"

The dog danced around him, whining with a mixture of caution and excitement. Apparently, Spot here was the only set of eyes that had been watching him through the trees. The poor thing wore no collar and needed a good brushing to clean the twigs and cockleburs from his dark gold fur. Feeling a tug of remembrance for the dogs his family had always had growing up, Trent held out his hand in a fist, encouraging the dog to get familiar with his scent. "You've been out here awhile, haven't you, little guy?"

Of course, standing six foot five made most critters like this seem little, and once the dog stopped his manic movements and focused on the scent of his gloved hand, Trent knelt to erase some of the towering distance between them and make himself look a little less intimidating. When he opened his hand, the dog inspected the palm side, too, no doubt looking for food, judging by the bumpy lines of his rib cage visible on either side of his skinny flanks. The stray wanted to be friendly, but when Trent reached out to pet him, the dog jumped away, diving through a snowdrift. But as if deciding the big, scary man who had no food on him was more inviting than the chest-deep cold and wet, he came charging back to the sidewalk, shaking the snow off his skinny frame before sitting down and staring up at Trent.

"What are you saying to me?" Trent laughed again when the dog tilted his head to one side, as though making an effort to understand him. "I'm Trent Dixon, KCPD. I'd like to ask you a few questions." The more he talked, the more the dog seemed to quiet. He thumbed over his shoulder toward the auditorium. "You know what happened here? Have you seen a curvy brunette and a little boy about yea high?" When he raised his hand to gesture to Tyler's height, the dog's dark brown eyes followed the movement. Interesting. Maybe he'd had a little training before running away or getting tossed out onto the street. Or maybe the dog was just smart enough to know where a friendly snack usually came from. "Your feet aren't big enough to make those tracks on the other side of the bridge. And I'm guessing you spend a lot of time around here. What do you know that I don't?"

The dog scooted forward a couple inches and butted his nose against Trent's knee. When he got up close like that, Trent could see that the dog was shivering. With his stomach doing a compassionate flip-flop, he decided there was only one thing he could do. Katie Rinaldi might not need rescuing tonight, but this knee-high bag of bones did.

"Easy, boy. That's it. I'm your big buddy now." Extending one hand for the dog to sniff, Trent petted him around the jowls and ears with the other. When the dog started licking his glove, desperate for something to eat, he grabbed him by the scruff of the neck. Other than jumping to his feet, the dog showed no signs of fear or aggression. Maybe the mutt had made friends with enough college students that he didn't view people as a threat.

"I'm afraid I'm going to have to take you in," Trent teased, standing and lifting the dog into his arms. Craving either warmth or companionship, the dog snuggled in, resting his head over Trent's arm and letting himself be carried up the hill to Trent's truck. "I'll get you warmed up and get some food in you. Maybe you'll be willing to tell me what you saw or heard then."

The dog was perfectly cooperative as Trent loaded him into the cab of his truck and pulled an old blanket and an energy bar from his emergency kit behind the seat. "It's mostly granola and peanut butter but...okay."

Taking the bar as soon as it was offered, the dog made quick work of the protein snack. "Tomorrow I'll get you to the vet for a checkup and have her scan to see if there's an ID chip in you." He got a whiff of the dog's wet, matted fur when he leaned over to wrap the blanket around him. "Maybe they can give you a bath, too."

Trent shook his head as the dog settled into the passenger seat, making himself at home. "This is temporary, you know," Trent reminded him, starting the engine and cranking up the heat. "I'm a cop, remember? I'll have to report you."

Stinky McPooch raised his head and looked at Trent, as though translating the conversation into dogspeak. His pink tongue darted out to lick his nose and muzzle and he whined a response that sounded a little like a protest.

"Don't try to sweet-talk your way out of this. You owe me some answers. So what's your story? No warm place for the night? Anybody looking for you?" The dog tilted his head and an ear flopped over, giving his face a sad expression. Trent turned on the wipers and shifted the truck into gear before driving toward the street. "Sorry to hear that. I'm a bachelor on my own, too. You can call me Trent or Detective. What should I call you?" When he stopped at the exit to the parking lot, Trent reached over the console to pet him. Pushing his head into the caress of Trent's hand, the dog whimpered in a doggy version of a purr. "All right, then, Mr. Pup." He pulled onto the street. There wasn't much traffic this time of night, so it was safe enough to take his eyes off the road to glance at his furry prisoner. "Did you see anything suspicious at the theater tonight?"

The dog barked, right on cue.

When Trent moved both hands to the steering wheel, the mutt put a paw on his arm, whimpering again. Trent grinned and scratched behind the mutt's ears, loving how the dog was engaging in the conversation with him. "Tell me more. I like a witness who talks to me. I think you and I are going to get along."

His interrogation skills were intact.

Now if he could just get a certain brunette to tell him what the hell had panicked her tonight.

Chapter Three

Trent was a man on a mission when he stepped into his boss's office at the Fourth Precinct building. Lieutenant Ginny Rafferty-Taylor was out somewhere, but he'd spotted Katie going in earlier and wanted a few minutes of face-to-face time with her before the morning staff meeting started.

Instead of asking a pointed question about last night's phone call, however, he paused, unobserved, in the doorway as she dropped to the floor.

"Where did I put that stupid pencil?"

He did a poor job of keeping his eyes off the bobbing heart-shaped curves of Katie Rinaldi's backside as she crawled beneath the conference table in search of the accursed writing instrument. Thank goodness Lieutenant Rafferty-Taylor was nowhere to be seen, because he was failing miserably at professional detachment. He stood there like a man, not a cop, admiring the view, savoring the stronger beat of his pulse until Katie's navy blue slacks and the mismatched socks on her feet disappeared between two chairs.

With temptation out of sight, Trent's brain reengaged and he swallowed a drink of his coffee. The hot liquid burned a little more common sense down his throat, reminding him that he was at work, the fellow members of KCPD's cold case squad were gathering in the main room outside with their morning coffee and case files, and Katie had made it clear that—no matter how she twisted up his insides with this gut kick of desire—she only wanted to be friends.

I love you, Trent. I always will. But I'm not in *love with you.*

Man, had that been a painful distinction to make.

He'd felt an undeniable pull to this woman since he was fifteen years old and she'd moved in with her aunt across the street from the home where he'd grown up. Although he'd been a jock and she'd been into the arts, proximity and a whole yin and yang thing of opposites attracting had played hell with his teenage libido. When she'd gotten pregnant their senior year, his idealistic notions about the dark-haired beauty had dimmed. But when she disappeared, and he'd played a small role in helping her get safely home, an indelible bond had been forged between them, deeper than anything raging teenage hormones could account for.

After her return, she'd talked him into singing in a musical play with her and he'd discovered he liked driving her back and forth to rehearsals and hanging out with her. They'd dated a few times their senior year of high school. Well, he'd been dating, hoping for something more, but Katie had always pulled back just when things were getting interesting.

She didn't mean to be a tease, and had always been straight with him about her feelings and concerns. It just wasn't easy for her to trust. He understood that now better than he had ten years ago. She'd grown up with an abusive father, witnessed her mother's own murder at his hand.

She'd survived a kidnapping, but lost the good friend she'd been trying to help when she'd gotten involved with the kidnappers in the first place. She'd had an infant son before graduation and had to learn about being a mother.

Katie had every right to be cautious, every right to insist on standing on her own two feet, every right to protect herself and her son from getting attached to someone who'd thought he was going to make a career for himself in another city. She wouldn't risk the stability she provided for Tyler. She wouldn't risk either her or her son possibly getting hurt. He'd admired her for her stubborn strength back then. Still did. Understanding why she wouldn't give them a chance, Trent had accepted the dutiful role of friend and gone off to play football in college and take his life and dreams in a different direction. Some dreams died or morphed into other goals. He'd come back to Kansas City, come home to be a cop.

He might be a different man than the teen he'd once been. But the rules with Katie hadn't changed. One wiggle of that perfectly shaped posterior, one flare of concern that all was not right in her world, shouldn't make him forget that.

Besides, a man had his pride. Yeah, being built to play the defensive line made him a little scary sometimes. But he wasn't completely unfortunate in the looks department. He had a college degree and a respectable job, and his parents had taught him how to treat a lady right. He didn't have to pine away for any woman. He dated. Okay, so a lot of those dates—like Erin Ballard last night—had been set up by Katie herself, but he could get his own woman when he had to. He'd even been in a couple of long-term relationships. It wasn't as if he was a saint—he enjoyed a woman's company.

Trent drank another, more leisurely sip of coffee, cooling his jets while he remembered his purpose here. He anchored his feet to the carpet, bracing himself. From the grumbling sounds beneath the table, Katie was on a tear about something this morning. A civilized conversation might not be possible. But he'd gotten information from less cooperative witnesses in an interrogation room. He just had to stay calm and make it happen.

A chair rolled across the utility carpet as she popped out on the other side of the table. "You and I need to talk," Trent stated simply.

Her head swiveled around and her blue eyes widened with a startled look, then quickly shuttered. She knew he was talking about last night. But she blithely ignored the issue between them. "I have to find that pencil first." It was hard to feel much resentment when her bangs flew out in a dozen adorable directions after she raked her fingers through the dark brown waves and stood. "It's the second one I've lost today. I don't have time for this. I'm making my presentation to you guys this morning and—"

Trent tapped the back of his neck, indicating the bouncy ponytail where an orange mechanical pencil had been speared through her hair.

She buzzed her lips in a frustrated sigh and pulled the pencil from her hair. "Thanks."

He stepped into the room to keep their conversation private from their friends gathering outside the office. "You called me—"

"Trent, please." Katie gestured to their team leader's empty desk. "I have to get everything ready for the meeting before the lieutenant gets back."

Fine. He'd ease into the questions he had for her. As long as he could get her talking to him. Trent glanced over at the empty desk where the cold case squad's team leader usually sat. "Where is she?"

"The lieutenant got called into Chief Taylor's office for an emergency meeting. She said she'd be back in time for the team briefing."

"Emergency?" That word and news of an impromptu meeting with the lieutenant's cousin-in-law, aka the department's top brass, wasn't something a cop wanted to hear at the beginning of his shift. He eyed the other members of the team through the glass window separating Lieutenant Rafferty-Taylor's office from the maze of detectives' desks on the building's third floor. Max Krolikowski, his partner, along with Jim Parker and Olivia Watson, stood together chatting, apparently as unaware as he as to what the emergency summons might be. Katie's frenetic movements weren't exactly reassuring. "Any idea what's up?"

"Not a clue." She unplugged a cord, inserted a zip drive and pulled a file on her laptop. When she looked up at the dark television screen at the opposite end of the conference table, she groaned and circled around the table to fiddle with the TV. "It's not my job to keep track of every bit of gossip that comes through the KCPD grapevine. The lieutenant was heading out when I came in. She told me to go ahead and set up for the staff meeting. So, of course, the wireless connection is on the fritz, and I had to track down extra cords. Then I realized I left one of the files in my bag and hadn't uploaded the pictures yet, so I had to go back for that. And now the stupid TV—"

"Take a breath, Katie."

"*You* take a breath," she snapped, spinning to face him. "Really? That's your witty repartee?"

"I mean…" Her eyes widened like cornflowers blooming when her gaze locked on to his.

Accepting the remorse twisting her pretty mouth as an apology, Trent crossed the room to inspect the closed-circuit television. He tightened a connector on the side of the TV and turned the screen on for her. "There. Easy fix."

"Thanks." She bent over her laptop, resuming her work at a more normal pace. "I'm sorry. That was a dumb thing to say. I was going on like a chatterbox, wasn't I?"

"There's something buggin' you, I can tell. But it's just me, so don't sweat it."

"I'm not going to take advantage of your cool, calm collectedness. You didn't come to work so you could listen to me vent."

"But I do want to hear about last night."

She arched a sable-colored brow in irritation. Okay. Too soon to press the subject. Just keep her talking and eventually he'd get the answers he needed.

Trent reached around her to set his coffee and notebook in front of the chair kitty-corner from hers. Although Katie was of an average height and curvy build, she'd always seemed petite and fragile. It didn't help that she'd kicked off her shoes beneath the table, while he'd tied on a pair of thick-soled work boots this morning to shovel his sidewalks, blow the snow off his driveway and walk the dog he'd taken in around the block. Despite her uncharacteristic flashes of frustration and temper, and the static electricity that made the strands of her ponytail cling to the black flannel of his shirt, she seemed pretty and dainty and far too female for the cells in his body not to leap to attention whenever he got this close to her.

"You seem a little off your game this morning." He spoke over the top of her head, backing away from the enticement of making contact with more than a few wayward strands of hair. "You know something about the lieutenant's emergency meeting that you're not telling me?"

"Nope. She was business as usual."

"Is Tyler okay?"

"He's fine. I swear." Katie tilted her gaze up to meet his, confirming with a quick smile that that much, at least, was true. Then she went back to work on her laptop. She swiped her finger across a graphic on her screen and loaded the image of several mug shots up onto the larger screen. "I guess he's a little ticked at me. There's this stray dog that he's gotten attached to running around the theater this past week. He wants a dog so badly, it's at the top of his Christmas list. But our landlord won't allow pets. I mean, the dog is friendly enough, but he's skin and bones. I feel so bad for him, especially in this weather. Apparently, Tyler's been feeding him."

"A tan dog with a white stripe around his neck?"

"Yes. How did you…?" Her cheeks heated with color as she tilted her face up to his. "You went to the theater last night. I told you everything was fine."

Trent propped his hands at his waist, dipping his head toward hers. He matched her indignant tone. "No, you told me you'd *handle* whatever it was. If everything is fine, you wouldn't need to handle anything."

"Well, I don't need you to rescue me every time something scares me."

"What scared you?"

She paused for a moment before waving off his concern and turned back to her computer. "That's not what I meant."

"Then give me some straight answers. Something hinky was going on outside that theater. Either you saw something, or you at least suspected it." He wrapped his fingers around the pink wool sleeve of her sweater and softened his tone. "Something that *scared* you, and that's why you called me."

She hesitated for a moment before shrugging off his touch. "You were on a date."

"The date was over."

"Because of me?" She turned in the tight space between the table and chair, her forehead scrunched up with remorse.

He tapped the furrow between her brows and urged her to relax. "Because I wanted it to be."

She batted his hand away, dismissing his concern. "Trent, I don't have the right to call you whenever I need something. I'm not going to wimp out on being a strong woman and I don't want to take advantage of our friendship. We shouldn't have that you're-the-guy-I-always-call-on kind of relationship, anyway. You need to…find someone and move on with your life."

"I'll make my own decisions, thank you. I call you when I need something, don't I?"

"Sewing a button on your dress uniform is hardly the same thing."

"Look, you and I know more about each other than just about anybody else. We've shared secrets and heartaches and stupid stuff, too. That's what people who care about each other do. Now—as a friend who doesn't appreciate phone calls that make him think something bad has happened and he needs to drop everything without even taking a shower and speed across town in a snowstorm—"

"You didn't—"

"—I need you to tell me exactly why you called last night. And don't tell me you were frightened of that sweet little dog, who, incidentally, is spending the day at the vet's office while the Humane Society is checking to see if he's been reported missing."

Her eyes widened again. "You rescued the dog?"

"You wouldn't let me rescue you. Now answer the question. What scared you last night?"

"Nothing but my imagination. I'm sorry I worried you. The dog's okay?"

She changed topics like a hard right turn in a high-speed chase.

Trent shrugged. This woman always kept him on his toes. "I fed him some scrambled eggs and gave him water. He spent the night whimpering on a blanket in my mud-room, but he didn't have any accidents. Don't know if he's housebroken or just too scared he'll get into trouble and get dumped out someplace again. I took him to the vet's this morning for a thorough checkup and a much-needed grooming. My truck still smells like wet, stinky dog."

"Thank you." Her lips softened into a beautiful smile. When she reached out to squeeze his hand, he squeezed right back. "Thank you for saving him. I wanted to, but I'm not sure Tyler would understand having to take him to a shelter instead of taking him home."

"It looks like I'll be fostering Mr. Pup for a while. Until the Humane Society can find out if there's an owner or put him up for adoption. Maybe Tyler can come visit him."

Katie shook her head, whipping the ponytail back and forth. "Don't tell him that. He'd be at your house every day after school."

"You know I don't mind having Tyler around."

"I know. But… Mr. Pup? Tyler calls him Padre."

Trent nodded. The name fit. "Like a priest's collar. That's what I'll call him, then. Now, about last night…" He could do the sharp right turns, too. But her frustrated huff warned him he'd have to coax the answers out of her, just like he'd coaxed Padre into trusting him. "You have to give me something, Katie. You know I won't quit."

"I know." Her blue eyes tilted up to meet his briefly. Her gaze quickly dropped to the middle button of his shirt, where she plucked away what was most likely a couple of dog hairs. The nerves beneath his skin jumped as her fingers danced against his chest. But he couldn't allow himself to respond to the unintended caress. This was distraction. Nervous energy. Something on her mind that kept her from focusing. There was definitely something bothering Team Rinaldi this morning. "I have to get ready for the meeting."

"Every morning, you've been bragging about Tyler and the play you guys are doing. This morning, all you're doing is apologizing and fussing around like it's your first day on the job." Outweighing her by a good hundred pounds wasn't the only reason he wasn't budging. He covered her hand with his, stilling her fidgeting fingers. "Talk to me. Use words that make sense."

"Calling you was an impulse," she conceded. "Once I got my act together, I realized I shouldn't have bothered you."

Nope. He still wasn't budging.

Trent felt the whisper of her surrendering sigh against his hand. "They didn't need me backstage last night, so I was doing some work on my laptop out in the theater auditorium. I found a connection between an old double missing-person case and some new stuff we're working on. I got caught up following the trail through the reports and I lost track of the time."

This was remorse talking, maybe even a little fear, he thought, as she slowly tilted her gaze to his again. "I couldn't find Tyler when I was done. I mean, eventually I did. He was by himself in the parking lot, waiting for me. Everyone else had left and he was locked out of the building. And then I thought I heard... I swear someone was..."

"Someone was what?" He gently combed his fingers through her scattered bangs, smoothing them back into place.

"I thought someone was watching me. The lights went out, so it was pretty dark, and while I was looking for Tyler in the dressing rooms, some guy pushed me down and ran outside."

Trent's fingers stilled. His grip on her hand against his chest tightened. "A man attacked you? Are you hurt?"

She brought her other hand up to pat his, urging him to calm the blood boiling in his veins. "This is why I don't tell you things. It wasn't an attack. The dark always freaks me out a little bit, and my imagination made things seem worse than they were. Once I found Tyler with Padre, everything was fine."

"You don't know what that guy was after."

"He wasn't after me. Maybe I interrupted a break-in. Or some homeless guy snuck in to get out of the cold and he got scared by the blackout, too. He just wanted me out of his way so he could escape. Doug Price is going to give me grief tonight for not picking up the mess I left in the dressing room, but I wasn't hurt. I was more worried about Tyler."

He didn't care about whoever Doug Price was, but if he gave Katie grief about anything, he'd flatten him. "Did you report it?" She hadn't. "Katie—" His frustration ebbed on a single breath as understanding dawned. "You called *me*." Hell. He should have investigated inside the building instead of letting the dog distract him from his purpose. He should have gone straight to Katie's apartment when he didn't find her and Tyler at the theater, even if it was the middle of the night and he woke them out of a sound sleep. "I'm sorry. If I'd known what kind of danger you were in—"

"It wouldn't have done any good. By the time I found Tyler and went back to take a couple of pictures, anything suspicious I'd seen was gone." Katie quickly extricated her hands from his and nudged him out of her way. "I wasn't in any real danger. I was being a lousy mom last night. Guilt and reading that file about the missing teen and her baby made me imagine it was something more." She picked up a stack of briefing folders and distributed them in front of each chair around the table. "Except for that message."

Oh, he had a bad feeling about this. "What message?"

She tried to shrug off whatever had drained the color from her face. "Some prankster wrote something creepy in the snow behind the theater."

"And then he swept it away."

Katie spun to face him. "Yes. But how did you…? Right. You were there. And you don't quit."

He propped his hands at his waist. "What did the message say? Something about breaking in to the theater?"

She hugged the last folder to her chest. "I don't know if it was even intended for me."

"What did it say?" he repeated, as patiently as he'd talked to Padre.

"'Stop or someone will get hurt.'"

He dug his fingers into the pockets of his jeans, the only outward sign of the protective anger surging through him. "Stop what? Who'll get hurt?"

Her shoulders lifted with silent confusion. She didn't

have those answers. "Maybe he thought I was chasing him. I wasn't. The darkness freaked me out and kept me from thinking straight, and all I wanted to do was find Tyler to make sure he was safe. If I hadn't panicked, I'd have handled things better, and I wouldn't have ruined your evening."

Trent plucked the folder from her grasp and set it on the table. "You lost track of your son. That's supposed to frighten a parent. Don't beat yourself up about it. You said he's okay, right?"

She nodded. "We're both fine. Thanks for worrying."

"Thank you for sharing. Now maybe I won't worry so much."

She moved back to her computer and manipulated the pictures again. "I'll believe that when I see it."

They *did* know each other well. "Honey, you know I'm always going to worry—"

"You shouldn't call me *honey*." Katie glanced toward the window to the main room. "The rest of the team is here. I need to finish setting up."

Chapter Four

If that woman worked any harder at pushing him away, she might as well slam Trent up against the wall. "At least promise me you'll keep a closer eye on the people around you. If somebody was lying in wait for you—"

"I promise. Okay? Just let it go." Katie stepped around him as Max, Olivia and Jim came in, their animated conversation masking the awkward silence in the room.

"You're killing me here, Liv," Trent's partner, Max, groused. "A Valentine's Day wedding? You're already making me shave and rent a tux."

Olivia breezed past the burly blond detective, the oldest member of their team, taking her seat at the table. "Just because you and Rosie eloped to Vegas doesn't mean the rest of us don't want to share that special day with friends and family."

Max jabbed his finger on the tabletop, defending his choice in wedding arrangements. "Hey. I wanted to make an honest woman out of Rosie. And you know how her last engagement turned out. She wasn't interested in dragging out the process any more than I was."

Max's new wife had barely survived the nightmare of her first engagement to an abusive boyfriend and had become a recluse as a result. Meanwhile, Max had been fighting his own demons when the two had first met and clashed during the investigation into her ex-fiancé's unsolved murder. Mixing like oil and water, it was a wonder the prim and proper spinster and the rugged former soldier had ever gotten together at all. But Trent had never met two misfits who were a better match for each other. Max brought Rosie out of her shell, and she'd uncovered a few civilized human qualities that Trent's rough-around-the-edges partner had lost in the years he'd been dealing with post-traumatic stress. Max had been shot twice and Rosie nearly drowned solving that case. But the close calls had made them willing to risk everything and seize the love they'd found.

Trent might be a little envious of his older friend settling into the sort of relationship he'd once wanted with Katie Rinaldi, but he was happy for his partner. And he had been honored to fly out to Las Vegas to stand up for the couple.

"As soon as the doctor cleared me to travel, I made the reservations. There wasn't time to send out invitations." Max reached over to thump Trent's shoulder as he pulled out a chair to sit beside him. "At least I took the big guy with us."

Trent grinned, thinking he'd better join the teasing banter before anyone questioned the tension between him and Katie. "And then you put me on a plane back to KC twenty minutes after the ceremony so you two could get started on the honeymoon."

Max grinned. "Hey, I'm ugly. Not stupid."

Olivia was smiling suspiciously, working her cool logic on Max. "Maybe, since you cheated Rosie out of the whole white-wedding thing, she'd like to put on a fancy gown and see you all dressed up for once in your life. I've yet to see a man that a tuxedo couldn't make look good."

"I'd love to see her in a beautiful dress like that." Was the old man on the team blushing? Who'd have thought? Still, Max grumbled, "You're determined to make me miserable, aren't you?"

Jim Parker grinned and pulled out the chair beside his partner. "Maybe he's worried you're going to make him dance with you at the reception, Liv—after Gabe, your dad and your brothers, of course."

"And Grandpa Seamus," Olivia added. She pointed to Max. "But you are definitely on my dance card after that." She wiggled her finger toward Trent. "You, too, big guy. You all agreed to be our ushers, so it's tuxes and bouton-nieres for everyone."

Max put up his hands in surrender. "There's only so much froufrou a man can take, Liv."

Jim propped his elbow on the arm of his chair, lean-ing over to back up Olivia. "I don't know, Max. There are few things I like better than slow dancing with my wife. Natalie's pregnant enough now that when we're close, I can feel the baby kicking between us."

Max scrubbed his palm over the top of his military-short hair and muttered a teasing curse. "Okay, Parker. Now you've gone too far, buying into all of Liv's roman-tic mush." Knowing full well he was going to eventually buy into it, too, Max turned back to the lady detective. "I thought you were a tomboy."

Olivia smiled wistfully. "My wedding day will be the exception. I'm the only female in my family. You don't think those boys all want to throw a big party for me? Dad insists on me wearing the veil of Irish lace that Mom wore at their wedding, and I want to. It's a way of honoring her

memory and making me feel like she's there with us."
The mood around the entire table quieted out of respect
for Olivia's mother, who had died when she was just a
child. But the detective with the short dark hair didn't let
the room get gloomy. "Besides, Gabe looks gorgeous in
a tux, and I refuse to have him looking prettier than me."

"Impossible," Max teased. "But if you're going all for-
mal, then I guess I can put on a tie."

"Thank you for your sacrifice." Olivia smiled before
turning her attention to Trent. "What about you? Will
we see you dancing the night away at the reception?"
She snapped her fingers as an idea struck. "You should
bring Katie."

The brown ponytail bobbed as Katie's head popped up
from her laptop screen. "Me? Like a date?"

Trent groaned inwardly at the pale cast to her cheeks.
Did she have to look as if the possibility of attending a
friend's wedding together was such an out-of-left-field
idea?

"If you want." Olivia chided the low-pitched whistle
and sotto voce teasing from Jim and Max before smiling at Katie. "Stop it, children. Believe me, I understand
better than most about the department's no-fraternization
policy. But even though we're part of the same team, technically, you work in two different branches—information
technology and law enforcement. Besides, I was thinking
practicality. Trent's an usher and you're still going to be
one of my bridesmaids, right?"

"Of course. I was honored you asked me to be a part of
the ceremony, but..." Katie's apologetic gaze bounced off
Trent and back to the bride-to-be. "I was going to bring
Tyler as my date."

Olivia seemed pleased by that answer. "Even better. I'd

love to see the little man again. All three of you should come together."

Even though they hadn't gone out on a date together in nine years, it seemed as though everyone thought of Trent and Katie as a couple. Maybe the others even took it for granted that they were destined to be a family unit one day. The only people who knew it was never going to happen were Trent and Katie themselves.

Sinking into his chair, Trent took another long swallow of his coffee. He watched the strained expression on Katie's face relax as the two women talked about Tyler. Her round face and blue eyes animated with excitement as they wagered whether her nine-year-old son would make as much of a fuss about dressing up for the special occasion as Max had. Katie was a different woman when she talked about her son. Her eyes sparkled and the tension around her mouth eased into a genuine smile.

No wonder she'd been so upset about losing track of Tyler last night. Tyler was her joy, her reason for being— her number-one excuse for shunning Trent and any other relationship that threatened to get in the way of taking care of her son. It wasn't that she didn't care about Trent as a friend, but she'd given her heart to another male nine years ago.

Max's fist knocked on Trent's chair below the edge of the table. Trent took another drink before meeting his partner's questioning look. "You okay, junior? You're pretty quiet this morning."

"You're loud enough for the both of us."

Max grinned at the joke as he was meant to, but his astute blue eyes indicated he wasn't buying the smiles and smart remarks. "There's that whole tall, dark and silent thing you do, and then there's stewing over in the corner.

You two were duking it out in here before we came in, weren't you?" His gaze darted over to Katie and back to him. "Seriously, what's the problem? Is it you? Katie? Is the kid okay?"

Trent swore under his breath. There was no subtlety to Max Krolikowski, no filter on his mouth. When he saw a problem, he fixed it. When he cared about something or someone, he went all in. Hell of a guy to have backing him up in a fight, but best friend or not, Trent wasn't sure the man he'd been partnered with on the cold case squad was the guy he wanted to confide his frustration and concerns about Katie to. "She basically told me to mind my own business."

Max dropped his voice to a low-pitched grumble. "You think something's up?"

Even if Trent wanted to share his suspicions about blackouts and prowlers and threats in the snow, he wouldn't get the chance to. All conversations around the table stopped as Lieutenant Ginny Rafferty-Taylor rushed into her office. "Are we all here?" The petite blonde officer set her laptop and a stack of papers at the head of the table before going back to shut the door. "Sorry I'm late."

Trent set down his coffee and turned everyone's focus to the police work at hand. "Ma'am. Katie said you had an emergency meeting with Chief Taylor?"

The older woman nodded. "Seth Cartwright from Vice and A.J. Rodriguez from the drug unit were there, too. I'll get right to it since it affects investigations in each of our divisions."

"What affects us?" Jim asked.

"Leland Asher."

Trent's mouth took on a bitter tang at the mention of

the alleged mob boss whose name kept popping up in several of their unsolved investigations.

Olivia leaned forward at the familiar name. "What about him? Gabe's first fiancée was writing a newspaper exposé about Asher when she was killed." Olivia and Gabe had solved that murder, but they hadn't been able to prove Asher had hired the man who'd shot the reporter.

Even Katie, who had never dealt with Asher directly, knew who he was. "His name shows up as a person of interest in several investigations in the KCPD database. Has he been arrested for one of those cases?"

"Not likely," Max said. "He has a great alibi for any recent crimes. He's currently serving a whopping two years for collusion and illegally influencing Adrian McCoy's Senate campaign."

"Not even that, I'm afraid." Lieutenant Rafferty-Taylor shrugged out of her navy blue jacket, hanging it over the back of her chair before sitting. Her back remained ramrod straight. "Asher's case went to appellate court on a hardship appeal. The chief just got word that Asher is being released from prison early, on parole. That's what good behavior and a pricey lawyer will do for you."

A collective groan and a few choice curses filled the room.

"Any chance the judge made a mistake?" Trent asked.

Their team leader shook her head. "It's the holidays, Trent. I think Judge Livingston was feeling generous. Chief Taylor wanted to alert us that Mr. Asher will be back on the streets, albeit wearing an ankle bracelet and submitting to regular check-ins with his parole officer, sometime tomorrow or Thursday."

"Well, merry Christmas to us," Max groused, folding his arms across his chest. "Just what we need, a mob boss heading home to KC for the holidays. I bet the crime rate doubles by New Year's."

For a moment, the petite blonde lieutenant sympathized with her senior detective, but then she opened her laptop, signaling she was ready to begin their morning meeting. "I know we believe Leland Asher is the common link to several of the department's unsolved or ongoing cases. The chief wanted us to be fully informed so we can keep an eye on him. Without our efforts turning into harassment, of course," the lieutenant cautioned.

"I'm willing to harass him," Olivia volunteered with a sarcastic tone. Max pointed across the table and nodded, agreeing with the frustration-fueled plan. "What's the point of solving these old cases if a judge is going to let the perpetrators go with little more than a slap on the wrist?"

Trent could feel the tension in the room getting thicker. Cold case work wasn't an easy assignment. Sometimes evidence degraded or got lost. Witnesses passed away. Suspects did, too. Memories grew foggy with age. And perps who'd gotten away with murder or other crimes that hadn't yet reached their statute of limitations grew confident or complacent enough over the years that they weren't likely to confess. So when the team built a solid enough case to convict someone, it sure would be nice if they'd stay behind bars for a while.

"Are we moving any cases we think Asher might be a part of to our active files?" Trent asked.

The lieutenant nodded. "We should at least give them a cursory glance to see which ones to follow up on. I believe we can use this to our advantage. Katie, will you flag those files and send each of us copies for review?"

"Yes, ma'am." Katie's head was down and she was already typing. By the time she looked up to see Trent grinning at her geeky efficiency, she was hitting the send button. She smiled back before turning to the lieutenant. "I just ran a search for Mr. Asher's name, and all those files should show up on your computers by the time you get back to your desks."

Trent gave her a thumbs-up before turning back to the others. "It'd be a hell of a lot easier to prove Asher's connections to those crimes by seeing who he interacts with on the outside."

Lieutenant Rafferty-Taylor nodded to him, probably appreciating how his suggestion cooled the jets of the others in the room, especially his perennial Scrooge of a partner, Max. Then she gestured to Katie at the opposite end of the table. "Speaking of connections, Katie, you said you've come up with something we need to look at in your research? Shall we get to work?"

"Yes, ma'am." Katie shoved her bangs off her forehead and glanced around the table as everyone waited expectantly. Trent winked some encouragement when their gazes met. She smiled her thanks for his support before looking down at her laptop. She highlighted the first picture on the television screen and turned to point to the gathering of mug shots she'd posted there. "Detailed information is in the folder in front of you, but you can follow the gist of what I think might be a significant discovery up on the screen." As Trent settled in to listen to the presentation, the rest of them did, too.

"As you all know, Lieutenant Rafferty-Taylor has had me copying and downloading all of our old print files of unsolved cases into a database and cross-referencing them. There are still more boxes in the archives, but those are cases that are thirty years or older. I'm focusing on more recent crimes where the perpetrator and potential witnesses are likely to still be alive."

Max whistled. "You've already been through thirty years of open and unsolved cases? Hell, you're making the rest of us look like a bunch of goldbricks."

"Not a chance, Max." She laughed at the gruff man's teasing compliment. "I've been doing this pretty steadily since spring. And I didn't get shot up and have to go on sick leave, either."

Trent nudged his partner. "Or run off to Vegas to get married before reporting back for active duty." Katie's dedication explained a lot of her late nights and the pale shadows under her blue eyes. But was all this unpaid overtime she'd put in the reason she had no time for a relationship? Or was it the thing she chose to do to fill up the empty hours in her life so she wouldn't miss those relationships? "What did you find out?"

Katie curled a leg beneath her to sit up higher in her chair. "When Olivia was investigating Danielle Reese's murder last spring, she came up with her *Strangers on a Train* theory, and it got me to thinking."

Olivia nodded. "*Strangers on a Train*, as in the Alfred Hitchcock movie where two people meet and agree to commit murder for the other person."

Her partner, Jim, continued, "But since they've never met before and don't run in the same social circles, the one with the motive can arrange for an alibi, while the one who actually commits the crime won't pop as a suspect on the police's radar because he or she has no motive to kill the victim."

"That's why we arrested Stephen March for Dani Reese's murder." Olivia braced her elbows on the table and leaned forward. "The evidence says he's good for it.

But he had no motive. I still believe he was blackmailed into doing it, or—"

"He murdered her in exchange for somebody else killing Richard Bratcher," Max finished. Trent reached over and rested a hand on his partner's shoulder. March and Bratcher were sensitive subjects for the stocky detective because Stephen March was his wife's younger brother, and Bratcher had been the bullying fiancé who'd abused Rosie Krolikowski. Max nodded his appreciation at the show of support. "We got Hillary Wells for Bratcher's murder, even though she barely knew the guy." He turned his attention back to Katie. "Are you saying that you did your brainy thing and finally found where March and Dr. Wells could have met and set up their murder bargain?"

"Not exactly."

"What exactly are we talking about, then?" he asked.

"I designed a program to search for commonalities between cases by looking for key words or names or places. What I discovered is a pattern between several crimes that occurred over the last ten years."

"A pattern?" the lieutenant asked.

Katie nodded. "I haven't been able to prove that they're all linked to one particular case, or even to just one person, but I've made some interesting connections between these six suspects and—" she swiped her finger across her laptop, changing the images "—these six victims."

Trent recognized the pictures of both Dani Reese and Richard Bratcher, the victims Stephen March and Hillary Wells had killed. He also recognized the stout cheeks and receding hairline of Leland Asher. "It's not an exact swap where Suspect A kills Victim B while Suspect B kills Victim A. It's more as though they're links in a chain."

The lieutenant urged her to continue. "Do you have specific examples of those links?"

"Yes, ma'am." Katie adjusted the display to bring the twelve images up side by side before she twirled her chair to the side and got up to touch the television screen. Her ease in front of an audience reinforced Trent's suspicion that whatever had had her so flustered earlier had to do with the details about last night, maybe something that she still hadn't shared with him—not a presentation to her boss and coworkers involving multiple murders. "It's a painstaking process, but as I put in more information from the reports, I've come up with links from unsolved cases to people or events from murders you all have closed earlier this year. Some of these seem pretty random, but in a place the size of Kansas City, the fact that these people may have come into contact with each other at all seems compelling to me."

Olivia tried to follow Katie's line of reasoning. "Some of the connections are obvious. Stephen March killed Danielle Reese. Dani was investigating Leland Asher. Hillary Wells murdered Richard Bratcher, and he was the man who was abusing Stephen's sister, Rosie March."

Max swore under his breath. "Don't remind me."

She pointed to the photo of a distinguished white-haired gentleman. "This is Dr. Lloyd Endicott, Hillary Wells's former boss and mentor. He died in a suspicious car crash that has yet to be solved. We suspect he's the man Dr. Wells wanted to have killed, since she took over his company and the millions of dollars that went with it."

Although Trent sometimes worried that Katie's knowledge of all these dusty old cases bordered on the obsessive, he couldn't deny how useful it was to have a walking, talking encyclopedia working on their team. He pointed to the image of a professional woman with short dark hair. "Does Hillary Wells or any of those other suspects or victims connect to Leland Asher?"

Katie nodded. "You might be surprised to know that before she died, she worked out at the same gym Matt Asher does."

"Leland's nephew?" Trent shifted his gaze to the image of a young man in a suit and tie who wore glasses and bore a striking resemblance to Leland Asher. "You think the two of them knew each other?"

She shrugged. "I can't say for certain unless I dig into the gym's schedule, class and personal trainer files, but the opportunity to meet was certainly there."

"It would be easy enough to go to the gym and ask some general questions to see if anyone ever saw the two of them together," Trent offered.

The lieutenant nodded. "Make a note to do that."

"Yes, ma'am."

"I don't have any evidence that Hillary Wells and Leland Asher ever met." Katie pointed to the nephew and then to Leland Asher. "But Max discovered that Matt regularly visits his uncle in prison."

Olivia nodded. "I'm guessing he's in the family business, although we haven't been able to prove that he's guilty of anything illegal. But he's down in Jefferson City nearly every week, so you know he must be passing messages to and from his uncle. Leland could have ordered Hillary to kill Richard Bratcher."

Jim Parker agreed. "It'd make sense for Matt Asher to keep the family business running while Uncle Leland is incarcerated. Where are his parents? Is his father involved in any of Leland's criminal activities?"

"There's no father in the picture. I did a little research

through Social Services and found what I could on his mother. She's Leland's sister—never married. It's in your folders. Isabel Asher overdosed when Matt was eleven— ten years ago." Katie pointed to the image of a blonde woman who had probably once been a knockout before the blank, sunken eyes and sallow skin in the photograph marred her beauty. "That's why she was in the system— she was fighting an ongoing addiction to crack cocaine, was in and out of rehab. There were several calls from teachers about neglect. After Isabel's death, Matt Asher went to live with his uncle."

Max tipped his chair back and said what they all sus- pected. "The dope was probably supplied by her brother's import business. If not, he'd certainly have the money to buy her whatever she wanted."

Jim concurred. "Access to her brother's wealth would make her a prime target. Let me guess, there's a boyfriend she used to shoot up with. Asher blamed him for his sis- ter's death and that guy's in one of your dead files?"

"Well, Francisco Dona did have a couple of arrests in his packet, but he can't be involved in any of our more recent crimes." She highlighted the mug shot of a dark- haired lothario with long, stringy hair and a goatee. "He died in a motorcycle accident shortly after Isabel's death."

"Are we sure it was an accident?" Trent asked.

Katie drew a line from Francisco Dona to Lloyd En- dicott. "Well, even though one rode a motorcycle and the other drove a luxury car, the sabotage to the engines was similar."

"As if both crimes had been committed by the same person?" Max sat up straight, his gruff voice incredulous. "Wow, kiddo. You're thorough."

"It's a thing I do. I like to poke around. Solve puzzles. It's just a matter of getting access to the right database."

Lieutenant Rafferty-Taylor threw a note of caution into the mix. "And having the legal clearance to access that database?"

"Yes, ma'am." Katie's lips softened with a sheepish smile. "Either I've got departmental clearance or it's public access. I haven't needed a warrant to put together any of this information, although there are places I could dig deeper if I did have one. I've sent out feelers to businesses, doctors, private citizens and so on to update our records. Some are eager to answer questions and help. Others don't even respond. Of course, I could find out more if..." She twiddled her fingers in the air, indicating her hacking skills. Trent had no doubt that Katie could access almost any information they needed—but the way she'd obtain it wouldn't stand up in court and no conviction would stick.

The lieutenant smiled. "We'll work within legal means for now. Continue with your report. This is already good stuff we can follow up on."

Trent read through the slim report on the dead socialite. "Says here the detectives assigned to the case suspected foul play in Isabel Asher's death. They thought it might be a hit by a rival organization to send a message to Asher. So you think Francisco Dona made a deal with someone to kill her?"

Katie nodded. "There was no conclusive evidence in her KCPD case file, although that's an angle the detectives in the organized crime division investigated before it was closed out as an accidental death."

Olivia thumbed through the information in her folder. "You *have* been busy. These deaths all happened within a general time frame, six to ten years ago. It makes our *Strangers on a Train* theory plausible."

Jim dropped his folder on the table, shaking his head. "But there are six murder victims here. And we've only solved two of them. And we haven't linked either of those conclusively to Leland Asher ordering those murders. You said this guy is getting out this week. If we can't pin something solid on him, we'll never get him back in prison." The blond detective looked from the lieutenant back to Katie. "Is there any place else where all of their killers could have met with Asher? Even randomly?"

"You mean like sitting together at a ball game? I haven't found anything like that yet, but..." Katie sat back in her chair and drew lines from one picture to another on her computer screen, giving them all a visual of her extensive research. "Leland Asher was diagnosed with lung cancer two months ago. The doctors suspect he's been suffering longer than that."

Their team leader nodded. "That probably helped prompt his early release as well—so the state doesn't have to pay for his medical treatments. What else?"

"Either Matt Asher or Leland's girlfriend, Dr. Beverly Eisenbach, have been to see him every week while he's getting radiation treatments and chemo shots." Katie drew another line. "Matt and Stephen March both saw Dr. Eisenbach as teens for counseling. Hillary Wells ran Endicott Global after Dr. Lloyd Endicott's death, and Dr. Endicott belonged to the same country club as Leland." The grumbles and astonished gasps around the table grew louder as the links of this twisted chain of murder fell into place. "Isabel Asher was Leland's sister and Matt's mother, of course. Roberta Hays was the DFS social worker assigned to Matt's case. And..."

Trent looked up from the notes in his folder when she hesitated. "What is it?"

She circled the image of a haggard-looking man with graying hair. "I found a connection to me in here."

"What is it, kiddo?" Max asked, voicing the others' surprise and concern.

"Roberta Hays's brother is Craig Fairfax."

Ah, hell. Trent recognized the name from Katie's past. *That* was what had truly scared her. He sat forward, extending his long arm to the end of the table. He reached for Katie, his fingertips brushing the edge of the laptop where her hands rested on the keyboard. But she curled her fingers into a fist, refusing his touch. That didn't stop him from asking the question, "You discovered Fairfax in your research last night?"

Her gaze landed on his, and she nodded before explaining the significance of that name to the others. "He's the man who kidnapped me when I was seventeen. He tried to take Tyler from me as part of an illegal adoption ring. He and his sister Roberta—who used her position with Family Services to scout out potential candidates like me—are both serving time now."

No wonder she'd gotten obsessed with her work and lost track of both Tyler and the late hour last night. Trent was already sending a text of his own, verifying that Craig Fairfax was still locked up in a cell in Jefferson City and not running loose on the Williams College campus.

"What's his connection to cold case?" the lieutenant asked, gently reminding Katie of the focus of the team's investigation. "Does he fit in with our *Strangers on a Train* theory? Can we tie him to Asher's criminal organization?"

Katie nodded. "Mr. Fairfax was diagnosed with prostate cancer earlier this year." She drew one last line on the computer screen from one sicko to another. "He's in the same prison infirmary with Leland Asher."

Chapter Five

"You need me there to back you up?" Max Krolikowski's voice was a deep growly pitch over the cell phone Trent slipped beneath the edge of his black knit watch cap as he climbed out of his truck at the Williams College auditorium.

"Nah, brother," Trent answered, flipping up the collar of his coat against the clear, cold night. He turned his back to the bitter wind blowing from the north and strode across the cleared pavement toward the massive brick building. "This is personal. We're off the clock."

"Doesn't mean I won't be there in a heartbeat. I owe you for helping me keep an eye on Rosie this summer." Max chuckled. "Besides, I decided I like ya. I'd hate to have to break in a whole new partner."

Trent laughed, too. "Nobody else would have you, you grumpy old man."

"Bite me, junior."

"Love you, too." Stretching out his long legs, Trent stepped over the snow piled between the sidewalk and curb. He noted that the parking lot was crowded with cars and the pavement and sidewalk had been cleared from one end to another by plows. There'd be no footprints to follow tonight unless the perp he believed had been spying on Katie was dumb enough to trek through the drifts. But if the guy who'd shoved her to the floor was that kind of dumb, Trent intended to be here to have a conversation about keeping his distance from the Rinaldi family. "Hey, did you ever hear back from the gym Matt Asher belongs to?"

"I thought we were off the clock."

"I'll stop thinking about these unsolved cases when you do."

Trent's booted feet quickly ate up several yards walking around to the front lobby doors of the building while Max grinched around in the background. When his partner came back to the phone, Trent knew he'd been checking the facts in his notebook. "Since the manager didn't seem to know much when we visited this morning, I stopped by on my way home and chatted up the after-work crowd. Several people recognized Matt Asher and Hillary Wells, but couldn't remember if they'd ever seen them in a conversation with each other."

Trent figured with the discrepancy between their ages—Matt barely being twenty-two and the late Dr. Wells being a professional woman in her forties—that any conversation more intimate than a polite greeting between the two of them might stand out enough to make an impression on at least one of the other gym members. When he suggested the idea, Max concurred. "Asked and answered. No one I spoke to could recall either Matt Asher or Hillary Wells being in the same room together, much less sharing that they were looking for a way to have someone killed."

The sharp wind bit into Trent's cheek when he turned to the front doors. He hunched his shoulders to stay warm. "So that's not our connection between the two of them.

Still, eliminating the gym doesn't mean she didn't have some other connection to Leland Asher."

"So we keep digging."

Trent nodded. "I'll ask Katie if she's come up with anyplace else that can tie the two of them together."

"Or tie Dr. Wells directly to Asher." Trent heard a soft voice in the background, then something that sounded suspiciously like lips smacking against each other. Max's gruff tone softened. "Rosie says to tell you hi—"

"Hey, Rosie."

"—and invite you over for dinner sometime before Christmas."

"I accept. Will you be there, too?"

"Wiseass." Trent grinned at the reprimand he heard in the background. "Um, the missus says I need to mind my manners. Maybe Friday before we all go see the little man in his play?"

"Sounds like a plan."

"Give me a call sometime to let me know if anybody else tries to bother Katie. She's part of the team, too. I don't like the idea of anybody messin' with one of us."

"That's why I'm here. If nothing else, I'm going to make sure she and Tyler aren't the last ones here and walking by themselves to their car again." Trent held open one of the glass front doors for a pair of chattering, bundled-up coeds who must have been leaving an evening meeting or practice in one of the fine arts classrooms. He barely saw their bold smiles and flirty eye contact. He silently bemoaned the idea that their interest in him sparked amusement rather than any fraction of the pull that a few ponytail hairs clinging to his shirt had that morning. "Ladies," he acknowledged to some silly giggles before they hurried past him and he signed off on his call to Max. "I'll keep you posted."

As soon as he stepped into the lobby out of the wind, Trent pulled off his cap and stuffed it into a coat pocket along with his phone. He removed his gloves and unzipped his coat before heading across the worn marble floor to the auditorium's dark red doors.

He stooped a little to peer through the cloudy glass window near the top of the door and saw a hazy tableau of the Cratchit family lifting their pewter mugs in a toast. He smiled when he spotted the little boy with the old-fashioned crutch tucked beneath his arm. Tyler's smudged face was easily the most animated of all the children onstage as he said his lines. There was a lot to admire about Katie's son. Trent didn't remember having that much confidence at that age, except maybe playing sports—but certainly not speaking in front of an audience. "Way to go, Tyler."

Trent shifted his gaze to the sloping rows of seats in the shadows between the lobby and the brightly lit stage. There wasn't much of an audience to be nervous about tonight. There was a skinny, graying man in a turtleneck pacing back and forth between the curved rows of seats. There were some obvious family of the cast scattered around, one running a handheld video camera, another snapping pictures with her phone. And there sat Katie beside a pile of coats in a chair in the middle of it all. Her downturned head made him think she was working on something in her lap instead of watching the rehearsal. Her laptop? Didn't that woman ever take a break from work? Was there something obsessive about learning the truth about that long-missing girl? Or was Katie reading more about Craig Fairfax, the man who'd tried to steal an infant Tyler from her and murdered her high-school pal Whitney Chiles?

"Come on, Katie Lee." His low-pitched whisper reverberated against the glass. She carried the weight of too much life experience on those slim shoulders. She didn't need to take on any more trouble. "Just enjoy the show."

If Katie was going to put in overtime making sense of the cases the team was working on, then he should do the same. Remembering his main reason for driving out here tonight, Trent detoured up the stairs to the tech booth in the balcony. He pulled out his badge before knocking on the door. The two men inside running lights and sound seemed willing enough to chat.

"Detective Trent Dixon," he identified himself, learning the men's names were Chip and Ron. "You guys know anything about a power outage here in the auditorium last night?"

"Yeah, I heard about the blackout," Chip, a balding man in metal-framed glasses, answered. "And how Katie foiled a break-in. But that's not on me. I locked up the booth when I left. And the work lights in the auditorium and backstage were still on. I walked out with Doug Price, the director. He turns everything off when he leaves— after the cast and crew are gone."

Only an innocent woman had been left behind in the dark. "Is there a way to turn off the work lights but turn on the rope lights to see backstage?"

Chip pulled down the lights at the end of the scene, then raised them slightly for the stage crew to come on and change the set for the next scene. Then he nodded. "The rope lights just plug in. Unless there was a power outage and everything in the building was dead, it'd be easy enough to throw a few switches backstage yet leave those on."

So the details Katie had shared about last night meant the blackout was deliberate. But whether the intent had been to trap her inside the theater or to cover up an intruder's escape, it was impossible to tell. "Did you see any signs of someone tampering with your light board?"

"It was just like I left it."

Ron, the sound guy with his cap sitting backward on his head, agreed. "The booth was locked up tight when I came in at six to set the microphones for rehearsal tonight. If anybody was in here, he had to have a key."

"And the director is the only person in the play with a key?" Trent would make a point of introducing himself to Doug Price.

Ron shrugged. "Except for campus security. Or maybe someone in the theater department. But all their productions are done for the semester. That's why we can be in here now."

The crew left the stage and both Chip and Ron went back to work. "Lights up."

Trent thanked them for their cooperation and went back down to the auditorium, sneaking in the back while Ebenezer Scrooge and the ghostly Spirit of Christmas Future walked onstage. After his eyes adjusted to the semidarkness, he spotted Katie's hot-pink sweater and headed down the aisle toward her. When he got closer, he could see that she was looking at a crumpled piece of paper instead of the flat screen of her laptop.

So she wasn't working. But her head was down and she was rubbing her fingers back and forth against her neck beneath the base of her ponytail, as if a knot of tension had formed there. She was so intent on whatever she was reading that she jumped when he slipped into the seat beside her.

"Sorry." He nudged his shoulder against hers to apologize for startling her, then nodded toward the paper she was quickly folding up. "What's that?"

"What are you doing here?" She dropped her voice to a whisper to match his before turning to the coats beside her. "Oh, shoot. I left my bag backstage." Without missing a beat, she stuffed the paper inside the pocket of her coat.

Okay. So that wasn't suspicious. He eyed the navy wool coat where the letter had disappeared. If that was some kind of threat… "Everything okay?"

"What? Oh." She pulled her lime-green scarf from the pile and folded it neatly on top of the coat, burying the missive beneath another layer. Right. So they were back to her keeping secrets and suffering on her own when he knew damn well he could help. "It's Tyler's letter to Santa. He said he doesn't believe in Santa Claus anymore but that he wrote the letter for my sake. I've always sent one out for him…mostly so I can read it and see what's tops on his wish list."

It was a plausible explanation for the frown between her brows. "That's a hard transition to go through the year they stop believing in the magic and hope of Christmas."

The frown eased a tad and she leaned toward him so they could talk without their voices carrying up to the stage. "He's still got plenty of hope, judging by the extent of that wish list. But other than some bad grammar, he sounds…" She sank back against the chair on a whispery sigh. "In a lot of ways he's still my little boy. But in some ways he's growing up way too fast."

Trent stretched out and slipped a friendly arm across

the back of her seat. "That growing-up stuff is inevitable. You do know that, right, Mom?"

She gave his ribs a teasing tap with her fist. "I know. And it certainly beats the alternative." That brief glimpse of a smile quickly faded. "When I think of some of those cases I've read through this year, like that missing teenage girl and baby—like my friend Whitney back in high school—I know we're lucky to be here. But I can't help thinking I've cheated him somehow, that I haven't given him everything he needs, that he feels he has to be all grown-up to take care of me. He doesn't, of course. But maybe he doesn't believe that I can take care of him."

"You're a terrific mom, and he knows that. All little boys want to try on being a man for a while, especially when they know they've got someone there to back them up in case the experiment isn't as exciting or safe as they thought it would be." Trent dropped his arm around her shoulders and pulled her to his side in a friendly hug. "To-morrow, he'll be a kid again. I promise." When she leaned against him, her fresh-as-a-daisy scent drew his lips to her hair and he pressed a kiss to her temple.

"Don't do that." Her hand at his chest pushed him away and she sat forward in her seat, moving away from the touch of his arm, as well. "If Tyler sees, I don't want him to get the wrong idea about us."

"The wrong idea?" Well, hell. "That peck was just a show of support between friends. A woman is damn well gonna know when I intend my kiss to mean some-thing more."

She turned with a surprised gasp. "Trent, I didn't mean to insult—"

He put up his hand to silence her apology. Yet when his gaze fell on the naturally rosy tint of her lips and lingered, the spike of resentment firing through his blood blended with a yearning he hadn't acknowledged in years. She shouldn't draw that pretty mouth into such a tightly controlled line, and he shouldn't have this urge to ease it back into a smile beneath his own lips. Maybe he had crossed a line without realizing it. Because, right now, every male cell in his body was wishing for a little privacy so he could kiss her just once the way he'd always longed to. But he hadn't had the skills as a teenager, and as an adult he didn't have the permission to even try.

For a long time now, he'd imagined if they could share one real, passionate kiss, he'd find out that this desire simmering in his blood was just the remnants of a teenage fantasy. He'd discover the spark wasn't really there. He and Katie would share a laugh over the awkward encounter, and he'd finally be able to get this useless attraction out of his system. Inhaling a cautionary breath, Trent pulled his hand back to rest on the arm of the seat, letting his shoulder form the barricade she wanted between them.

"It won't happen again." At least, he hoped he could keep that promise. "I'd never do anything to jeopardize my friendship with you or Tyler."

But as Trent faced the stage again, adjusting his long legs in the narrow space between the rows of seats, his eyes were drawn to the show's director, Doug Price. The pacing had stopped and the older man's dark eyes were trained on the seats where he and Katie sat. Tyler wasn't the only one she needed to worry about seeing and misinterpreting a quick kiss.

So, did the temperamental artiste simply dislike the hushed tones of a whispered argument near the back of the theater interfering with him watching his play? Or was there something more personal in the territorial sneer he aimed at Trent and Katie? Did this guy have a thing for Katie?

The flare of jealousy was fleeting, there to acknowledge but quickly dismiss. If there was one thing Trent understood about Katie Lee Rinaldi, it was that it wasn't *him* she was loath to have a relationship with. She didn't want a relationship with any man.

There was no competition here. Trent acknowledged the man's displeasure with a nod and scrunched down in his seat in an unspoken assurance that he wouldn't disrupt the rehearsal again.

But there were even curiouser things afoot when he noticed the Grim Reaper wannabe onstage repeatedly tugging on his mask, using the adjustment of his costume to peer out at the director. And, though it was impossible to track the exact direction of the actor's glare beneath the black hood and mask, Trent would bet money that the guy was taking note of Doug Price's interest in Katie, too.

Trent leaned his head toward Katie and whispered, "Who's the guy onstage?"

She guessed he wasn't talking about Mr. Scrooge. "Christmas Future is Francis Sergel. I made his costume. He's probably getting ready to complain about something that itches or doesn't fit him." She finally relaxed and settled back into the seat beside him. "He's good at that."

"Complaining?"

"Oh, yes." He grinned at the subtle sarcasm that bled into her tone. Although it still rankled that she would have such a strong reaction to that innocent kiss, Trent appreciated her attempt to return them to their normal footing with each other. He wasn't about to completely drop his guard and relax, though, not with the director and twitchy man onstage each sliding them curious looks. "So what's

on Tyler's list? You know I like to get the little guy a present every year."

He felt the momentary stiffening in her shoulder where
it brushed against his, but she didn't try any awkward
evasion of the question this time. "A bunch of video and
computer games. I'll give you a list. And a dog. If I'm
not careful, he's going to run away from home and move
in with you now that you're fostering Padre. That's *his*
dog. In his nine-year-old brain, anyway. He barely talks
about anything else."

"You know I've got two extra bedrooms at my house.
And a fenced-in yard. Tyler is welcome to come over to
visit anytime. They can play outside. That dog loves jumping and snuffling around in the snow. I think the cold in
his nose makes him a little hyper. He needs somebody
Tyler's age who can keep up with him. Heck, maybe I'll
even put Ty to work picking up Padre's messes in the
backyard."

Katie laughed out loud, then quickly slapped a hand
over her mouth when Doug Price swung around to glare
at her again. She quickly dropped her voice back to a
whisper. "Do it. That'd be the reality check Ty needs to
understand that owning a pet is a lot of work and responsi-
bility. It's not just the landlord's rules or me being mean."

"I'll make the offer."

"Douglas!" Trent sat up straight when Francis Sergel
jerked the black hood off the back of his head and stepped
out of character and walked to the edge of the stage. "I
can't work like this."

For a split second, Trent instinctively went on the defensive, worrying that his accusatory whine was targeted
at Katie. It wasn't until he felt her hands through the thick

sleeve of his coat that he realized he'd thrown his arm out in front of her.

Now, *that* was a look that warned him he'd overstepped the boundaries between them again.

Francis pulled the mask off his face and shook it at the director. "This needs another elastic strap sewn in. It keeps shifting on my face and I can't see."

Doug Price turned his face toward the catwalk near the ceiling and griped, "Spare me from working with these dime-store divas," while the actor playing Ebenezer muttered something similar. Then the director swung around and snapped his fingers. "Katie. Grab your sewing kit and take care of that."

The squeeze of her hands around his forearm kept Trent from answering back about talking to her in that dictatorial tone. Apparently, Katie hadn't been singled out, because the director used the same tone with the actor onstage. "Give your mask to one of the crew, Francis, and finish the scene."

"I need the mask to get into my character." The bearded man with black circles drawn around his eyes needed more than that Grim Reaper robe and makeup to get his creepy on?

"All you have to do is hit your blocking marks and point. Rise to the challenge." Doug gestured to the temperamental actor, then turned again. "Katie? Sooner rather than later, if you would. I'm trying to get an accurate running time on the show tonight."

"My sewing kit is in my bag in the greenroom."

"Then get it." His gaze slid past her to Trent. "And this is a closed rehearsal. Tell your boyfriend to buy a ticket if he wants to watch."

That's it. The need to stand up to that idiot jolted

through Trent's legs. But Katie's hand on his shoulder and a warning look kept him in his seat. She stood and beamed a smile at the director. "He already has."

Trent could have choked on the honey dripping from her voice, but the sweetly veiled retort seemed to appease Mr. Price. With a nod to Katie, the director turned back to the actors onstage. "All right. Let's take it back from your entrance, Francis."

He hissed a whisper behind her back as she moved in front of him toward the aisle. "So kissing you on the head is off-limits, but letting your director think I'm your boyfriend is okay?"

"That's Doug's interpretation, not mine. He saw your picture with Tyler on my computer and..." She looked down at him, her mouth twisted with another apology. "I didn't correct his mistake. Misleading Tyler is one thing. But sometimes, Doug is a little friendlier than I—"

"How friendly? Someday you're going to have to explain the rules—"

"Mom?"

Trent heard the loud whisper from the corner of the stage and peeked around Katie to see Tyler's smudged face peering from the edge of the heavy velvet curtain. The tiny dimple of a frown appeared between his feathery eyebrows, reminding him of Katie when she was stewing over a problem. Had he heard Price yelling at her? Had he seen the two of them arguing? Did he think he needed to protect his mama?

"Douglas? Now I have to deal with this?" When Mr. Death up there pointed to the little boy showing his face onstage, Trent shot to his feet, grabbing Katie on either side of her waist and moving her to his side. If he turned that snooty temper on Tyler...

But Katie Lee Rinaldi had already made it clear she could protect her son her own self, thank you, very much. "It's okay," she said in full voice. She stayed Trent's charge to her defense with a hand at the middle of his chest. She nodded to the actors and stopped the director before he could open his mouth. Then she curled her thumb and finger into an okay sign and winked to her son. "I'll be right there."

When she tapped either corner of her mouth and modeled a smile for him, Tyler's moment of concern disappeared and he smiled back at her. The boy smiled at Trent and thrust his hand out at waist level, sneaking a not-so-subtle wave to him. Trent put his fingers to his forehead and returned a salute, offering his own reassurance that the child didn't need to worry about his mom or anyone else while he was here.

As quickly as he'd popped out, Tyler disappeared behind the curtain.

"And this hobby is fun for you?" Trent dipped his chin to meet Katie's whispered thanks.

"The creative part of it is. But on this production, some of the people…" Katie's gaze shifted back and forth between Price and Sergel. "Not so much. But don't go all alpha on me. I can handle Doug and Francis. I already know how to deal with children."

His throat vibrated with a chuckle at her sarcasm. "Yeah, but yours behaves better."

Her fingers tangled together with his in a quick squeeze. "Duty calls. Thanks for stopping by. I know Tyler is happy to have you here to watch him. Although I think you make him a little nervous."

Trent tightened his grip to stop her as she scooted past him, surprised at the admission. "I do? I don't mean to.

The whole team is coming to opening night. Will he be okay with that?"

She smiled away his concern. "Relax. Having a few nerves onstage is a good thing. Seeing you will keep him on his toes. He wants to do a good job for you."

Katie made it impossible not to smile back. "Tyler's always first-string in my book."

"He knows that."

"Katie!" Doug yelled. "I need this fixed before the next scene." Trent released Katie's hand and straightened to all six feet five inches of irritated man before shrugging out of his coat and hanging it on the back of his seat, making it clear without saying a word that he was staying and that the lashing out at her needed to stop. The director seemed to rethink whom he could push around by adding a succinctly articulate, "If you please."

"Trent…" She knew what he was doing.

"Go on. I'm doing this very beta style, I promise. I'm just going to sit here until the show's done so I can give Tyler my critical opinion."

"And make sure these guys mind their manners?"

"It's what a boyfriend would do, isn't it?" Trent doffed her a salute, too. He also intended to be here to walk her to her car after rehearsal was done and to make sure nothing *weird* happened tonight. He folded his big body into the seat as if it was the most comfortable chair in the world. "I know Tyler will be my favorite thing about the play."

"Thank you." She turned into the aisle and hurried down to the stage.

Frankly, he wouldn't put up with the bossy overlord and the whiny string bean onstage. But he was here to support Katie and Tyler, not to audition or volunteer backstage for anything himself. All the more reason to find out who had trapped her in the theater and separated her from her son last night. If it was just one of these bozos trying to intimidate her, his presence could put a stop to that. And if it was something more sinister, then the scene of the crime was the best place to look for the answers Katie wouldn't give him.

Like what was in a letter to Santa that could upset her like that?

Once Katie took the mask from the stagehand and disappeared behind the curtain, Trent reached across the empty seat into her coat and pulled out the letter that had dented a worried frown on her smooth forehead. If that story had all been a lie and it was some kind of threat related to last night, and she didn't think she needed to tell him, then... He read the addressee on the envelope out loud. She hadn't lied. "Santa Claus?"

He pulled out the crumpled letter and smoothed it against the thigh of his jeans before reading.

Dear Santa,

I think you might not be real. My friend Wyatt says that his mom is Santa Claus but I know you are not a girl. I'm writing this letter just in case because Jack says your real, and because Mom asked me to write you a letter and it makes her happy when I do what she says. If you do come by on Christmas Eve, I want a dog, a cell phone, the action figures from the movie I saw this summer, gamer cards and a dad. Uncle Dwight is fun to do stuff with, but he is cousin Jack's dad. Jack is in second grade at my school and is fun to play with. Jack's not really my cousin, but it's weird to have an uncle younger than me and Dwight's more like a grandpa. Mom says

our family dynamite is complicated. I want a dad
who can play baseball and computer games, but I
don't want him to be so good that he beats me all the
time. Mom won't let me play any battle games, but I
like the racing games and the ones where you have
to collect stuff and get speshul powers. I found a
dog named Padre at rehersal. He can be mine if you
want. If you can catch him. He likes peanut-butter
sandwiches. A dad with a dog would be the best.
Your friend,
Tyler Rinaldi
PS: I live in an apartment, so you will have to come
in the front door because we don't have a chimney.
I can leave it unlocked.
PSS: Jack wants a racing car set and boxing mitts.
PSSS: I don't want one of those little girlie dogs
with a bow in her hair.

A dad? Tyler had asked Santa for a dad? No wonder
Katie had fretted over the letter. There were at least two
things on this list she couldn't give her son, and that had
to be difficult for a single mom who wanted to give the
world to her child. And yeah, Tyler did sound a little like
a cynical grown-up in a couple places. But this was still
the voice of a little boy speaking from his heart.

Trent felt a few sentimental pangs pulling on his heart,
too. He'd known Tyler since the boy was an infant and
his neighbor Maddie McCallister—now married to DA
Dwight Powers—had taken the rescued baby in to care for
him until she and Dwight had tracked down the missing
Katie and broken up that illegal adoption ring.

The illegal adoption ring headed by Craig Fairfax.
Craig Fairfax, the man who'd ordered the murder of

their high school classmate Whitney Chiles. The man who'd tried to kill Katie, and Maddie and Dwight, too.

Craig Fairfax, the man who shared a prison infirmary with reputed mob boss Leland Asher, the prime suspect in several of the unsolved cases their team was investigating.

If Katie's thoughts had taken the same dark trail, then she was probably more worried, unsure and afraid than she was letting on.

Trent's nostrils flared with a deep, quiet breath as the cop in him took over once more. He was here to keep Katie and Tyler as safe as they'd let him and to put a name to any threat that might mean them harm. Whether that threat was a frightened intruder; a cast or crewmate with some kind of bitter feelings or obsession toward Katie or Tyler; a convicted killer who might be using a mob boss and his connections to take revenge on the family who'd put him away for life; or even the mob boss himself, who was taking advantage of the inside knowledge he could gain on Katie in some bizarre plan to thwart the cold case squad's investigation into him and his activities—he couldn't leave the family alone and unguarded. No matter how awkward things got between him and Katie, no matter how angry she got at his interference—no matter how painful it was for him to be close and not have what he'd once wanted—he wasn't going anywhere.

The Rinaldis and finding answers to this complicated mix of unsolved cases were his number-one assignment now.

Trent carefully returned the letter to the pocket of Katie's coat and smoothed everything back into place. Then, while the Spirit of Christmas Future and Ebenezer Scrooge resumed their journey through the bleak future that awaited a man who refused to change his miserly ways, Trent pulled out his phone and sent a couple of queries to the KCPD database, checking to see whether Doug Price or Francis Sergel had any kind of criminal record or had been listed as a person of interest in any ongoing cases.

Interesting. Francis Sergel's name didn't show up anywhere until about ten years ago on a DMV app, and the guy had to be in his late forties or fifties. That most likely meant a legal name change for any number of reasons, from annoying enough people in his previous life and needing a fresh start to entering witness protection or something more nefarious. A man with only a recent past also meant a search through databases that Katie would have to access for him. But who would change his name to Francis? Or Sergel? Unless there was some kind of personal significance to the name. That was something else Katie could find quick answers to if he put her on the hunt.

And then there was Douglas Price. His fingerprints were in the system because he used to be a public school teacher. But there was nothing more than a few speeding tickets in his history.

Scrooge was dancing a jig with his nephew's wife and celebrating Christmas when a shadow fell over Trent.

"Don't get on my case about working when I'm off the clock if you're going to do it, too." Katie plopped down in the seat beside him, hugging her bulky canvas carryall bag in her arms. "Did something come up?"

Trent brushed his finger over his phone to darken the screen. "I was doing a little background check on a couple of your friends here." The dent between her delicate eyebrows instantly appeared. But he wasn't going to lie to her about his concerns. "Did you know Francis doesn't show up in the system until around ten years ago?" He nodded toward her bright green-and-blue bag. "You got something in that magic computer of yours that can tell me why he changed his name and who he used to be? Or at least give me an idea why he'd pick that name?"

"Francis?" She opened the flap of her bag and pulled out her laptop. "You think he's suspicious?"

"I'm a cop, Katie. I'm suspicious of everyone until I have an explanation that makes sense." He clipped his phone back onto his belt and rested his forearm on the chair between them. "I just want to make sure we've got nothing to worry about from any of the people around you."

"I told you last night I probably got in the way of an intruder."

"Then why mess with the lights? Why go to the extra effort to threaten you?"

"You think someone here... That Francis would...?" She pulled out a smaller remote gadget, turned it on and set it on the chair beside her. Then she dropped her bag to the floor and set her laptop on her knees. "Okay. What do you want me to look up? Legal cases? Witness relocation? Criminal profiling reports?" She reached over and tapped the back of his hand as she turned her open laptop toward him, urging him to look at the display screen. "Trent?"

"Son of a bitch." Trent felt his temperature go up, even as her fingers chilled against his skin.

There was a message scrawled in lipstick across the screen.

Stop what you're doing.

"That message last night *was* meant for me."

Chapter Six

Max Krolikowski strode onstage to join Katie, Tyler and the other members of the production company Trent had gathered to ask a few questions. Max dangled a plastic bag with a tube of lipstick inside. "I found this in the makeup supplies in the dressing rooms. The tip's worn flat and it looks like a match to the color on Katie's laptop. The case has been polished up, though." He glanced down at Katie, sitting in one of the dining table chairs on the set. "Either you guys are fanatics about cleaning up, or somebody's wiped it for prints."

She appreciated Trent's partner answering the call as soon as Trent had phoned and requested backup—"Somebody got to Katie again."

But right now she was wishing Max wasn't such a good cop and that the evidence relating to that disturbing message hadn't been so easy to find. Katie shook her head, not liking the implication. "We're not fanatics."

There was no longer a plausible option to dismiss the weird things that had happened to her at the theater. Someone was watching her. Someone was taking advantage of the opportunity to frighten her. And he was succeeding. She'd made a life for herself behind the scenes now—at work, at the theater—putting her son first. Being thrust into the spotlight by an anonymous stalker didn't feel so good.

Trent thanked the mother who'd been taking pictures with her phone and dismissed her and her daughter. "Let's take the tube, anyway. Maybe the lab can get a latent or DNA off it or the laptop." His big shoulders lifted with a shrug that Katie didn't find very reassuring. "So far, everybody's been cooperative, but no one saw anyone or anything that seemed out of place backstage. That makes me suspect someone here, whose presence wouldn't be questioned. Someone who's better at lying than I am at detecting it. I'm not sure where to take this next."

"You'll figure it out, junior. We just keep asking questions," Max advised, dropping the lipstick into the paper sack where her computer had already been tagged and bagged as evidence. He rolled up the top of the sack, then paused when he saw Katie watching him. "You're okay if I do this, kiddo? Will you need this for work tomorrow? I know you and your computer are attached at the hip."

Attached at the hip, hmm? Apparently, not closely enough.

"It's okay, Max," she assured him. "I ran a quick diagnostic myself. It doesn't look as though anyone messed with any of the files or programs, and I have everything backed up on a portable hard drive. Plus, I have a desk computer at home and at work."

Katie rubbed her hands up and down her arms, trying to erase the chill beneath her cardigan and blouse. She couldn't help but let her gaze scan the faces of the remaining cast and crew sitting onstage or in the audience seats. Had the makeup kit from the dressing rooms merely been an item of opportunity for an outsider? Or was someone involved with the play a better actor than anyone suspected? And what did any of this have to do with her?

Trent's cool gray eyes passed over her, winking a silent version of *hang in there* before he turned to Doug Price and repeated the question he'd already asked. "Did you see anything that looked out of place earlier this evening? Anyone you didn't recognize?"

Doug's grayish-blond eyebrow arched up with disdain. "Besides you?"

Max folded his arms over his sturdy chest. "Answer the question."

Perhaps thinking better of crossing the detectives who'd taken over his rehearsal, Doug eased his taut features into an imitation of a smile. "Look, I'm as concerned about Katie's safety—about the safety of everyone here—as you are, Detective. The entire cast and crew were here tonight. In fact, I think it's the first time since we started rehearsing that no one's been absent because of illness or a conflict. The kids all have a parent or guardian who comes to rehearsals with them, too. I won't allow any of the little minions to be unsupervised."

"So you're saying there were more people than usual here tonight," Trent clarified. "And you knew all of them?"

Doug considered his answer for a moment before crossing to the edge of the stage and pointing to the back corner of the auditorium. "There was a man here filming the scenes with the children. I'd never seen him before. I assumed he was a father who'd come instead of the moms who are usually here."

"Oh, my God." Katie's stomach twisted into a knot. There'd been a strange man filming Tyler and the other children? She instantly sought out her son, playing a card game with Wyatt on the stairs leading down to the seats.

He must have felt her concern because he looked up at her and frowned. Damn it. She was worrying him again. Better than most, she knew what it was like to be afraid for a mother's safety. She shouldn't be scaring him.

A large hand closed over her shoulder. She glanced up at the sudden infusion of warmth and support. But Trent was asking her for information as much as calming her fears. "Did you recognize this man?"

Her gaze drifted out of focus, trying to visualize the man she'd only glanced at in passing. "I didn't know him. But I assumed the same thing—that he was someone's dad."

"Can you describe him?"

"The camera was in front of his face when I saw him. Brown hair. Brown wool coat. Um, dress shoes instead of snow boots." She blinked her eyes back into focus. "His camera was a digital Canon with a mini zoom lens. Black woven strap around his neck. Sorry, that still doesn't give you a name or face."

Trent grinned. "Leave it to you to notice the tech. And don't apologize. This is a lot more than I knew a second ago." Even as he jotted down the limited description, she saw him checking the people remaining in the theater. Katie didn't see anyone who matched her vague description, either.

"Trent?"

A tug on Trent's sleeve turned him away from her. Katie watched her son's eyes tip up to the man who towered above him.

"What is it, buddy?" Trent dropped to one knee, putting himself closer to eye level with Tyler. "Do you know the man I'm asking about?"

Tyler shook his head. "There wasn't any dad here

except for Kayla's. She gets to stay with him this month, and it was his turn to watch us backstage. He doesn't have much hair at all."

Trent nodded at the matter-of-fact explanation. "What's Kayla's dad's name?"

"Mr. Hudnall."

When Trent glanced back at Katie, she filled in the blank for him. "Willie Hudnall. We all signed up to take different nights to supervise the children backstage. He was in the greenroom with the kids when I went back to fix Francis's mask."

"So he was there when your laptop was unprotected. He could have written that message there."

She hated to think the man she'd been grateful to for checking on Tyler twenty-four hours ago might now be a suspect. "My point is, I would have recognized him if he'd been the man in the audience. We all would have. Plus, Mr. Hudnall was wearing hiking boots, not dress shoes."

Max nodded to Trent and pulled out his phone. "I'll give the description we have to campus security. Find out if they've seen anyone like that."

While Max took a few steps away and made the call, Katie gestured to the others remaining for this official Q and A. "There are more than two dozen people backstage at any given time. More if you count the crew. Any one of them could have…" She pulled Tyler onto her lap and hugged her arms around him. She looked again. Looked closer. Maybe the enemy was right here. A friend in disguise. One of the people she trusted—one of the people she trusted with her son.

Trent rose in front of her, reading her distress. "Any one of them could have left you that message."

"But why? What am I doing that's such a threat to

anyone? I'd rather think it was that stranger. I know these people. I've been hanging out with them almost every evening for weeks now. Some of them have become friends." She shoved her fingers through her bangs, willing some sort of clarity to reveal the truth. "What does it mean? What am I doing that I have to stop?"

A noisy harrumph from the front row drew Trent's attention. "You got something to say, Mr. Sergel?"

Francis might have cleaned off his makeup, but wearing street clothes as black as the costume he wore in the play, and taking the stairs two at a time on his long, spidery legs, he still bore an ominous look that would keep Katie from ever trusting the man. "Just that Ms. Rinaldi keeps flirting with our director."

"Excuse me?" What was wrong with this guy to give him such a petulant mean streak? "I don't flirt with anybody."

Although he spoke to Trent, his beady, dark eyes were focused squarely on Katie. "Maybe someone resents that she's drawing attention to herself and trying to make her or Tyler Doug's favorite."

Katie shot to her feet, holding on to Tyler's shoulders to keep him from tumbling to the floor. "Are you kidding me? I haven't done anything to make Doug think—"

"Doug's the one who keeps hitting on Mom," Tyler piped up.

The director's head swung around, as if he'd dozed off during the part of the conversation that didn't concern him. "I beg your pardon?" He took a step closer. "I was simply being friendly. You keep to yourself so much, I wanted you to feel included."

"My mom doesn't even like you, and you're too old to be a dad," Tyler argued. "You should leave her alone."

"Tyler!" More shocked by her son's choice of defense than by Doug lying about his interest in her, Katie turned him to face her. "What do you know about men hitting on women?"

"Mo-om." Tyler rolled his eyes. "I watch TV. I know stuff. And I watch you, too. Doug's always asking you to go somewhere after rehearsal."

"And I always say no."

Trent stopped the mother-son conversation with a hand on her arm and turned their attention back to Francis. "Are you jealous, Sergel?"

"I only have the best interests of this production in mind."

"If the boss is paying more attention to the pretty lady than to the show onstage, that bothers you?"

"Well, of course it does. I think it bothers all of us."

"So you have a problem with Katie and Mr. Price being friends," Trent reasoned. "Would you like her to stop doing that?"

Francis lifted his pointy chin. "I am not answering any more questions without my attorney present."

"Have you done something to make you think you need an attorney?" Francis was tall. But Trent was taller. And bigger. He forced Francis to take a step back just by leaning toward him. "Did you deface Katie's computer? Maybe wanted to teach her a lesson? Remind her of her place? You were backstage for most of the play."

"Stop twisting my words around."

But Trent Dixon didn't back down. "I saw you snap at more than one person tonight, including Tyler and Katie. Maybe you're the one who wants to be the director's favorite."

"I refuse to answer any of your accusations. I only want the best show possible, and these two amateurs—"

"We're all amateurs, Francis." Doug Price pulled Francis back beside him. "Stop talking before you say something you'll regret." He turned to the others watching from the audience. "Everyone, please. Detective Dixon, there are children here and it's late. May I send them home? This is all very upsetting and counterproductive to putting on a successful play, and opening night is Friday. I don't think you'll find out anything more tonight. You can get everyone's contact information from Katie's cast-and-crew list if you have more questions. No one knows who this man with the camera was, but I promise you, if he shows his face again, I'll demand he identify himself."

"I want to know what he took pictures of, too."

"Of course." Doug clapped his hands, ensuring that everyone was following his directions and moving toward the backstage exit. "Shall we? I'm sure campus security is waiting to lock up after us."

Trent nodded. "Tell them to go ahead. We'll be right out. Thank you to everyone for your cooperation." Although his smile included the cast, crew and parents filing past them, he had nothing but *I'm watching you* in his eyes for Francis, who didn't move until Doug gave him a nudge and a warning glare.

Doug himself was the last one of the interview group to leave the stage, but he paused and brushed his fingers against Katie's elbow. When she flinched, his grip tightened in a paternal squeeze, and she looked up into light brown eyes that seemed genuinely concerned. "I'm sorry this is happening to you, dear. I hope you'll do whatever is necessary to stay safe."

"Thank you, Doug."

He released her to give Tyler's chin a playful pinch. "Be sure to keep our Tiny Tim safe, too."

"I will."

Trent urged the director to follow the rest of the cast and crew. "Good night, Mr. Price."

Doug's cajoling smile disappeared. "Good night, Detective."

As soon as Doug had disappeared offstage with the others, Tyler rubbed his knuckles back and forth across his chin. "I hate when he does that. He treats me like I'm a little kid."

Salty tears stung Katie's eyes as her *little kid* showed yet another sign of growing up too fast. Despite his token grumble, she pressed a kiss to the crown of his hair and ruffled the dark curls before nudging him to the stairs. "Get your coat on and gather your things. Don't forget your library book for school."

She felt Trent's compassionate gaze on her but couldn't look up to meet it. Not without the tears spilling over. Refusing to turn into an emotional basket case of fear, fatigue and regret, Katie picked up her own coat off the back of the chair and slipped into it.

She was pulling her knit cap on when Max ended his call and rejoined them. "Campus security hasn't seen anybody matching Katie's description of the unknown man tonight, but they'll keep an eye open for anyone matching his general description. I took the liberty of encouraging them to track Sergel and Price's whereabouts when they're on campus, as well. I gave them the plates, make and model of their cars and texted the same to you, in case either one shows up someplace they shouldn't."

Trent was bundling up to face the wintry night, too. "You read my mind, brother. I'll follow up with Katie's list to see if anybody else jumps out as having some kind of motive." He thrust out his hand. "Thanks."

"I'm keepin' tabs on what you owe me, junior. Don't worry." Max laughed as he shook Trent's hand. "I'll make sure everybody else has left before I head to the lab." His goodbye included Katie. "See you two in the morning."

"Good night, Max. Thanks."

The burly detective dropped a kiss on her cheek. "Take care, kiddo." He exchanged a couple of fake boxing moves with Tyler. "You be careful, little man."

"I will. Bye, Max."

By the time the work lights were out and they said good-night to the security guard, Katie's car and Trent's pickup truck were the last two vehicles in the parking lot. Trent set Tyler's book bag in the backseat and knelt down in the open doorway to buckle him in and steal a quick hug while Katie stowed her own bag and started the engine. "You did a good job tonight, Tyler. For a while there, I forgot it was you onstage and thought you were Tim Cratchit. I can hardly wait to watch the whole show on Friday. I'll be sure to tell Padre what a good job you did, too."

"Padre?"

Trent grinned. "Yeah. Your mom told me that was the name you gave him. I picked him up last night. He's going to be staying with me for a little while, until he gets some meat on his bones."

Tyler made no effort to hide his gap-toothed smile—or stifle the yawn that followed. "Tell Padre I said hi. And that I want to come see him Saturday. And don't give him away to anybody until I get there, okay?"

"I won't. I'll tell him you're coming."

Katie looked across her son to the big man kneeling

there and mouthed, *Thank you*. Even though his eyes had drifted shut, her son was still smiling. She buckled herself in. "Good night, Trent."

But when Trent started to leave, Tyler's eyes popped open. "Mom? Do you think anything scary will be written on your computer at home?"

He must have been more aware of tonight's events—and more frightened by them—than she'd realized. She reached across the console to cup his cheek, hating that a nine-year-old should have a worry mark on his forehead. "No, sweetie. I don't see how anyone could get into our apartment. We'll be fine."

He roused himself from his sleepy state and sat up straight. "What if that man who took pictures of us is there? Can we call Trent if we see him?"

Katie was at a loss. How could she make Tyler's fears go away when she wasn't sure what was happening around her and whom she needed to be afraid of? "Sweetie, if you see that man...or anyone who... Of course, we'll call the police. I don't want you to be afraid. I—"

"And you'll stop doing whatever is making him so mad?"

She looked past those wide blue eyes into Trent's, wishing she knew how to answer Tyler's question. Trent's eyes had darkened like steel at the worried timbre in Tyler's voice. He reached into the car and palmed the top of Tyler's head. "Tell you what. I'll follow you and your mom home. Give the place a good once-over before you lock up. I'll make sure nobody's there who shouldn't be." He pulled his gloved hand into a fist and held it out to Tyler. "Sound like a plan, buddy?"

With a nod, Tyler bumped his small fist against Trent's and settled back into his seat.

Trent's gaze sought hers this time. "Are you okay with that?"

Okay with Trent reassuring her son and making sure they were both safe?

Katie nodded. "I'll see you at home."

Chapter Seven

Tyler's head had lolled over onto his shoulder and he was snoring softly in a deep sleep when Katie pulled into her parking space at the apartment complex where the two of them lived near the Kauffman and Arrowhead stadium complex. Trent had pulled into a visitor's space and joined them by the time she had her and Tyler's bags looped over her shoulder, and she was leaning into the car to unbuckle her son.

"Wait." A gloved hand closed around her arm and pulled her aside. "Let me." Trent took her place at the open door and reached in to lift her sleeping child into his arms. "Lock up and lead the way."

With a nod of thanks, she closed the door and locked the car. Then she reached up to tug Tyler's scarf and collar around his face to protect him from the cold night air. Katie was just as aware of Trent's bulky frame blocking the wind as he followed behind her as she was his constant scanning back and forth to ensure that no one seemed unusually interested in the trio coming home late at night. Trent's intimidating stature and the gentle surety with which he carried Tyler against his chest made her feel at once protected and a little nervous. She'd known the teasing Trent, the caring Trent, the solid-as-the-earth

Trent most of her life, and there was a deep comfort in that
familiarity. But there was a harder edge to the cop who
didn't back off from asking tough questions, his quick
ease at taking charge and asserting an authority that allowed no argument, a staunchness under fire that was
both exciting and a little unsettling.

Still waters run deep.

The observation lodged in her head and refused to re-
cede as she tapped her key fob against the lobby's auto-
matic door lock, and again to get inside to the bank of
elevators that would take them to the second floor. The
elevator doors closed and her nose filled with the crisp
scents of snow and cold on their clothes, the sweeter scent
of a little boy who'd eaten red licorice backstage in the
greenroom, and a muskier scent that was male and sexy
and not any kind of *boy* next door or old-friend-like in
the least.

What was wrong with her tonight? Had those threats
stripped away a layer of composure she needed to keep
her world in order? Why couldn't she stop analyzing the
subtle changes she'd noticed in Trent tonight? He'd ma-
tured into a powerful Mack truck of a man who bore
little resemblance to the lanky teen she'd once hung out
with. The shadow of his late-night beard emphasized the
angles and hollows along his cheeks and jaw. He moved
with the easy yet purposeful stride of a predator guard-
ing his territory. She'd gotten a glimpse of his temper tonight and been reminded that he was more complex than
the nice guy who could make her laugh or make her feel
safe. Had she just not allowed herself to analyze his size
and scent and changeable demeanor before? Why had
she overreacted to a simple kiss to her hair earlier? Why

should her curious mind be so fixated on the man riding silently in the elevator beside her?

Even seeing Trent step out of the elevator first to look up and down the hallway to make sure it was clear felt different than all the times she'd had him over for a home-cooked meal or a bit of mending in exchange for putting together a bike for Tyler's birthday or teaching him how to hit a pitched ball or helping her replace a headlight on her car. And when had his jeans started hugging those muscular thighs with every long, sexy stride? *Stop looking!*

Feeling something very close to lusty attraction, and uncertain she wanted to feel anything like that for any man, Katie darted around Trent with her key to get the door open. Her soft gasp of breath at the rustle of her wool sleeve brushing against his nylon coat was like a mental alarm clock, waking her from this ill-timed fascination with the man.

"Make sure it's locked before you insert the key," Trent whispered. "Any sign of a break-in and we're turning around."

Feeling less sure of her relationship with this version of Trent Dixon, Katie obeyed his direction. She twisted the knob and felt the solid connection there. "It hasn't been tampered with."

After unlocking the door and pushing it open, she waited for a few seconds after he carried Tyler past her and inhaled a deep, senses-clearing breath before bolting the door behind her. She bought herself another second to shake off this discomfiting awareness that fogged her brain by taking off her gloves and cap and tossing them on the kitchen table with their bags before following Trent down the hallway to the two bedrooms there.

Trent had Tyler's gloves and hat off and had her son

half sitting on the edge of the bed, half leaning against him. Smiling at the sweet picture of man and boy, and refusing to acknowledge the pang of feminine awareness that instantly warmed her body, Katie knelt beside them. With Tyler's head resting on Trent's ample shoulder, Katie peeled off his jacket and clothes and changed him into the superhero long johns he wore for pajamas.

Katie tucked Tyler under the matching bedspread and sheets and bent over to kiss his soft, cool cheek. "Good night, sweetie. Pleasant dreams."

"G'night, Mom," the sleepy boy muttered. "'Night, Trent."

"Good night, buddy."

Katie turned on his night-light before joining Trent at the open doorway. They watched Tyler for a minute or so until he sighed and rolled over, fast asleep, secure in his own bed. Exhaling her own sigh of relief, Katie backed out of the room and pulled the door to behind them. "Thank you for helping with him," she whispered.

"Never a problem." Trent stuffed his cap and gloves into the pockets of his coat as he followed her to the kitchen. She pulled out a stool at the counter and invited him to sit while she hung her coat, along with Tyler's, over the back of a chair. Then she opened the top of Tyler's book bag and pulled out his homework folder and the remnants of his lunch. Trent unzipped his coat and settled onto the stool while she checked to make sure Tyler had completed his schoolwork at rehearsal.

"Is it too late to offer you a cup of coffee?" she asked, making the effort to sound as normal as she would on any other night Trent visited, despite battling the disquieting urge to shoo him on out of the apartment so she could sort through all these feelings buzzing to the surface tonight and get herself back in order again. "A couple of cookies, maybe? We baked Christmas cookies with Aunt Maddie this past weekend."

"I'm not hungry." He took out his notepad and pen. "I thought of this on the drive over. Before I leave, I want you to check your bag again. Tyler's, too. I want to make sure I've got all the details before I write up my report."

Katie squeezed the brown lunch sack in her fingers and turned to him. "You don't think this is about me? You think he got into Tyler's stuff, too?"

Trent's eyes had cooled from that intense storm cloud from earlier in the evening to an ordinary, calming gray. "I've got no evidence to think that, but I know the best way to get to you is to do something to that little boy. So humor me, okay? I want to make sure I cover all my bases."

Any last chance at reclaiming normalcy vanished at the idea of Tyler receiving one of those disturbing threats. She immediately dumped the squished sack and sorted through a sandwich bag with bread crusts and pretzel bits and an empty applesauce container. She thumbed through the folder of papers, scanning each page to make sure there were no extra messages or bright red lipstick scribbled on one. Checking each pocket of the bag, she found the deck of gaming cards he had been playing with earlier at rehearsal. All the children took books and games to keep them occupied when they were backstage waiting to go on. "This looks like the normal mess I unpack every evening."

"Now yours. Is there anything missing? Anything that's been tampered with besides your laptop? Anything been added that wasn't there before?"

"Some loose things spilled to the bottom of the bag when he pulled the computer out. But it's all my junk."

Katie opened the matching navy, white and lime-green billfold and fingered through some ones and a twenty, along with the receipts she'd tucked in with them. She checked her debit and credit cards, pulling the cards half-way out of their pockets and pushing them back in. "I don't think whoever it was stole any..."

Katie's mind sorted through several snapshots of memories that hadn't meant anything at the time. She touched the clear plastic window where she kept her driver's license and a couple of punch cards for a local coffee shop and pretzel cart. Her shoulders tensed. Oh, no. No, no.

"What is it?" The wood stool creaked as Trent rose to stand beside her. "Katie?"

"These two punch cards are switched around, and the corner of this one is bent. I'm sure it wasn't before. And my license isn't centered like it was before. I think he pulled them out and stuffed them back in. He searched through my things."

"He pulled out your driver's license?" He reached around her to lift the billfold from her grasp and inspect the cards.

"Maybe." She looked up at him over her shoulder. "Do you think he was looking for my home address? If it was someone from the play, our numbers and addresses are already on the cast-and-crew list. Why would he need to check my license?"

"To throw us off the scent? Because he was gone the day Price handed out the contact list? Because he isn't a part of your show?" Trent muttered something under his breath. "Maybe because this twisted perp has some kind of obsession with you?"

Like the bitter wind blowing outside her windows, a chill swept through Katie, freezing her right down to the bone. "Obsession?" Hugging her arms across her waist, Katie shivered. "My father was obsessed with my mom. He didn't like her to be with anybody when he wasn't around. He barely tolerated her being with me. And when she tried to get away from him, to help me get away…" Joe Rinaldi had killed her mother. Katie's vision blurred with tears. "What if this guy shows up here or does something to Tyler?"

Katie was rattled. She was exhausted. And she was afraid. When Trent put an arm around her shoulders, she turned in to his hug. Pressing her cheek against the soft nap of his flannel shirt and the harder strength underneath, she slid her arms around his waist beneath his jacket and let the heat of his body seep into hers.

The other arm came around her at the first sniffle. "I won't let him hurt you, sunshine. I won't let him hurt Tyler, either."

She nodded at the promise murmured against the crown of her hair. But the tears spilling over couldn't quite believe they were truly safe, and Katie snuggled closer. Trent slipped his fingers beneath her ponytail and loosened it to massage her nape. "What happened to that spunky fighter who got her baby away from Craig Fairfax and helped bring down an illegal adoption ring?"

Her laugh was more of a hiccup of tears. "That girl was a naive fool who put a lot of lives in danger. I nearly got Aunt Maddie killed."

"Hey." Trent's big hands gently cupped her head and turned her face up to his. His eyes had darkened again. "That girl is all grown-up now. Okay? She's even smarter and is still scrappy enough to handle anything."

Oh, how she wanted to believe the faith he had in her. But she'd lost too much already. She'd seen too much.

She curled her fingers into the front of his shirt, then smoothed away the wrinkles she'd put there. "I'm old enough to know that I'm supposed to be afraid, that I can't just blindly tilt at windmills and try to make everything right for everyone I care about. Not with Tyler's life in my hands. I can't let him suffer any kind of retribution for something I've done."

"He won't."

Her fingers curled into soft cotton again. "I don't think I have that same kind of fight in me anymore."

"But you don't have to fight alone."

"Fight who? I don't know who's behind those threats. I don't even know what ticked him off. It's just like my dad all over again."

"Stop arguing with me and let me help."

"Trent—"

His fingers tightened against her scalp, pulling her onto her toes as he dipped his head and silenced her protest with a kiss. For a moment, there was only shock at the sensation of warm, firm lips closing over hers. When Trent's mouth apologized for the effective end to her moment of panic, she pressed her lips softly to his, appreciating his tender response to her fears. When his tongue rasped along the seam of her lips, a different sort of need tempted her to answer his request. When she parted her lips and welcomed the sweep of his tongue inside to stroke the softer skin there, something inside her awoke.

Katie's fingertips clutched at the front of Trent's shirt, clinging to the warm skin and muscle beneath. She tried to keep things simple, to indulge herself in a little comfort without forgetting the rules that kept her world in order. But with fatigue, charged emotions and the history between them to combat, the rules suddenly didn't make much sense, and the friendly embrace gave way to a real, passionate kiss.

Sliding her hands up, she smiled at the ticklish arousal of her palms skimming over the scruff of his beard. Trent tasted the width of that smile with his tongue before touching his padded thumb to the corner of her mouth and demanding she open fully for him. With a breathless moan in her throat, she obeyed. As he plunged his tongue inside to claim her, she was quickly consumed by the searing heat of his kiss.

Trent unhooked the band of her ponytail and sifted the falling waves through his fingers. For a moment, Katie thought they were falling. But she quickly found the anchor of Trent's shoulders as he sank back onto the stool at the counter and pulled her between his legs. Drawn to the heat that instantly flared between them, she pushed the cool nylon of his coat down his arms and moved in closer. He released her only long enough to shrug the coat off and let it fall to the floor before he gathered her close again. Katie wound her arms around his neck, and his hands slipped down to palm her butt, lifting her squarely into his desire, letting her body fall against his.

Katie melted into his strength. Tears were forgotten as she surrendered to the shelter of his arms and the forthright desire in his kiss. Each tentative foray between them was welcomed, rewarded. Surrounded by Trent's arms and body, cogent thought turning to goo by a sudden craving for his lips on hers, Katie felt her fears and a lifetime of worry and regret slipping away until there was only a man and a woman, and Trent's heat chasing away the chill of the long night. Such strength. Such gentleness. Such patient seduction. The mother in her went away. The weariness diminished. The loneliness disappeared.

Katie had been kissed before. She'd been kissed by Trent. But he'd been a teenage boy then. She'd been little more than a girl herself. This Trent was all grown man, with hard angles and knowledgeable hands. Her breasts grew heavy and pebbled at the tips, rubbing in frustrated need against the layers of clothing between them. His fingers tugged at the hem of her sweater and blouse, then slipped beneath to sear her skin. He palmed the small of her back, dipped his fingertips beneath the waistband of her jeans and panties to brand the curve of her hip. Denim rasped against denim as he adjusted her between his strong thighs and bulging zipper, stirring an answering need deep within her. This was a different kiss. A deeper kiss. It was a kiss that sneaked around her defenses and made her forget that she was anything other than a woman who hadn't been kissed or held for a very long time.

She reveled in his strength. The passion arcing between them jump-started her pulse and refueled her energy. His raw desire renewed her own confidence and strength. She needed this. She needed Trent.

"Katie," he gasped against her mouth. Her lips chased his to reclaim the connection. This wasn't the time for talking. She heard the deep-pitched chuckle in his throat even as he nipped at the swell of her bottom lip. "Sunshine. The counter's digging into my back. Can't we find someplace a little more comfortable?"

A woman is damn well gonna know when I intend my kiss to mean something more.

Her fingers stilled in the tangle of his hair. This wasn't right. Trent Dixon wasn't supposed to be so all-fired manly and irresistible. She wasn't supposed to want him like this. Katie turned her mouth from the sting of his lips and a kiss brushed across her cheek instead. She brought her hands down to brace them against his shoulders and put a little space between them. Her nerve endings seemed to be short-circuiting. She slid down his body until her toes touched the floor, but she wasn't sure her legs would hold her upright. There were reasons a kiss like this had never happened between them before. She'd forgotten what was important. She'd forgotten Tyler.

She'd forgotten the threats.

Katie needed the cop. She needed the friend. She couldn't afford to lose either one from her life right now.

Finally coming to her senses, Katie blinked his grinning mouth into focus and shoved at Trent's chest. "What was that?"

She would have staggered away if his hands hadn't settled at either side of her waist to steady her. "Maybe it's the way things should be between us."

"No." Her hands dropped to the bulk of his biceps and pushed again. "I'm not going to make any more mistakes."

Trent's grip on her tightened, as if sensing her instinct to bolt. "Where's the mistake, Katie? I know you have feelings for me. And I've never made any secret—"

"I care about you, Trent. But I'm not—"

"In love with me." What was left of his smile disappeared. He set her away from him and reached down to snatch his coat off the floor. He towered over her when he stood. The drowsy timbre of his voice hardened like his posture. "Trust me, I know the difference." She hugged her arms around her waist and stepped out of the way as he shot his arms into the sleeves and shrugged the coat over his shoulders. "That wasn't the kiss of a woman who only cares about a friend. Deny it all you want, but there's something between us."

"Don't do this, Trent. Please. Not now. I don't want to fight."

"This is an adult discussion, not a fight. Maybe I've been reading you wrong all these years, thinking you were just too scared, too wounded to trust anyone completely—that you just needed time to heal. Maybe patience doesn't pay off." He stalked across the kitchen and foyer to the front door.

Katie followed, hating that he saw her like that, like some kind of small, wounded bird. "I don't need you reading me at all. I just need you to leave before I say something I'll regret."

He halted with his hand on the knob and spun around, startling her back a step. "What would you regret, sunshine? You regret having my help tonight?"

"No."

He leaned in closer. "You regret kissing me?"

"Like that, I do. Yes." Katie put up a hand to ward off his advance and planted her feet. "I regret being impulsive."

Trent walked right into the palm of her hand, forcing a connection between them. When she would have pulled away, he caught her hand against his chest. He reached out to brush her hair off her face, his callused fingertips stroking her skin as he smoothed the wayward waves behind her ear. "That's one of the things I've always liked about you. You may be a brainy chick, but you always follow your heart." He laughed, but there was no humor there. "Except with me."

Katie tugged her hand free and backed away from the taunt she felt in his touch. "I can't afford the luxury of being impetuous anymore. I'm not the same person I was when I was seventeen and I thought I could save the world.

I can't afford to be. Not with Tyler in the picture." She crossed to the table and picked up the remains of Tyler's lunch and carried it around the island to stuff it into the trash. "You know how many mistakes that's gotten me into in the past. It's what got me kidnapped by Roberta Hays and Craig Fairfax. It's what got Whitney killed."

"Caring about people isn't why you and Whitney—"

"If someone is targeting me for a reason we haven't figured out yet, then it's all the more important that I keep my head about me and not lose my focus and put Tyler at any kind of risk."

"I would never hurt Tyler. I love him—you know that."

"Yes, and he loves you, too." Funny, the big brute didn't look one bit smaller or any less irritated with her with the quartz counter and width of the kitchen between them. She gripped her own edge of the counter and willed him to understand why she couldn't handle another kiss like that. "What if you and I try to be a couple and it doesn't work out? Other than Uncle Dwight, who's like a grandfather to him, you're the closest thing Tyler has to a dad."

"A dad?"

"You know you're a natural at it. You're that perfect mix of buddy-buddy and making sure the rules get followed. You make him feel safe. And I know what it's like to be a child who doesn't feel safe. I won't put him through that." She blanked her mind to the memories of her father's violent rages against her mother before the remembered fear and helplessness could latch on and draw her back to the past. "If you and I take a stab at a serious relationship and it doesn't work out, then it's going to ruin our friendship and you won't be part of our lives anymore. If that happened, Tyler would be crushed. So would I."

"Why are you so sure we wouldn't work?" Trent crossed to his side of the island. "How do you know?"

"Because I screw things up, Trent." There. He knew that about her, but he'd forced her to say it, anyway. He straightened at the bald statement, his quiet rigidity sucking the charged energy from the room. It was a clever trick she'd seen him use in an interview room, creating an uncomfortable silence that a person felt compelled to fill with an explanation. "It's my fault Mom died. And because I failed her, I thought I could redeem myself by saving Whitney. I jeopardized the life of my own unborn child to help a friend, and she ended up dead, anyway. I nearly did, too." Katie raised her hands in a supplicating gesture. "I can live with my guilt and grief. I might even be able to handle a broken heart if I had to. But that's me. I would never ask Tyler to pay for my mistakes."

His eyes darkened like the shadows of the dimly lit room. "And you think you and me would be a mistake?"

"I can't afford to find out." Her arms flew out as the depth of her concerns pushed aside reason. "Get mad. Storm out of here. I'm sorry I can't be what you want me to be, but please… Think about where I'm coming from and try to understand. I need you to be my friend, Trent. I need you to be the rock in my life you always have been. Tyler needs that, too."

He nodded, as if finally seeing her point. But the man wasn't an interrogator for nothing. He set down his gloves and stepped back from the counter to zip his coat. "What if it *did* work out between us? What if you're robbing us of the chance to be happy—to be a family? I could be a real father to Tyler. And you know I'd be a damn sight better husband to you than your father was to your mom."

Katie carefully considered her answer. She had no

doubt that Trent would make a wonderful parent to her son or any other child. And that kiss? She circled the counter and crossed to the door to throw open the dead bolt and usher him out before those lingering frissons of desire could catch hold again. Common sense had to prevail. She had to make the right choices this time.

"One thing about us, Trent, is that we've always been honest with each other. Screwing up relationships is all I've ever done. And I don't want to fail at us. It would hurt too much. I forgot myself tonight. I was afraid and you were there for me. But I have to think about the future. I'd never want to mislead you, and I would never forgive myself if Tyler got hurt."

"You're asking a hell of a lot from me."

"I know. And it isn't fair. But maybe if we never give in, if we never start…"

She splayed her fingers on the closed door in front of her, feeling as though she'd been caught in a trap of her own making. They already had given in. The mistake had already been made with that little make-out session. Maybe the hurt was inevitable.

"You aren't a screwup, Katie Lee Rinaldi." She felt the heat of Trent's body behind her. "I'm not storming out of here in a temper, I'm not going to abandon you and Tyler when you need me, and I'm sure as hell not going to hit you."

"I know you would never—"

"For what it's worth, your mother's murder wasn't your fault."

"But it was." She spun around, seeing nothing but a wall of dark gray coat. The grit of unshed tears rubbed at her eyes. She hadn't blanked the memories, after all. It had been cold that night, too. There'd been so much yelling, so much pain. So much blood. "If I hadn't skipped my curfew that night, Mom wouldn't have been out looking for me. I was the reason Joe got so mad, the reason he blamed her. And when he slapped me and she said that she'd had enough and we were going to leave him—"

A large hand palmed the nape of her neck, lifting her onto her toes. Then Trent's mouth was on hers again. This kiss was hard and quick, a forceful stamp that drove away the nightmare. His face hovered near hers when he pulled away, and Katie couldn't look away from those dark gray eyes. "Your father was a bully and a bastard, and I'm only sorry that there was no one to stop him from hurting you and your mother back then. But it was *not* your fault."

"Trent—"

He pressed a thumb to her lips to silence any further discussion. "*Not* a screwup," he repeated before nudging her to one side and pulling open the door. Maybe as stunned by his unflinching support as she was by the power of that kiss, Katie hugged her arms around herself, trying to hold on to the warmth he'd instilled in her while he tugged on his cap and gloves. "I have to go home and let the dog out. Lock up behind me. Try to get some sleep. I'm going to put you to work on some research in the morning. In the meantime, I'll make sure someone's watching the building through the night."

"Have I scared you off with my neurotic fruitcake-iness?"

"You won't get rid of me that easily, sunshine." He stepped out into the hallway. There was a trace of the familiar grin she'd grown up with when he glanced back over his shoulder. "Who'd have thought you'd be the one to come up with so many rules? But I'll follow them. For now. You and Tyler will be safe."

The door closed behind him and she threw the dead bolt. But she sagged against the painted white steel when the full promise of Trent's words registered.

For now.

What happened when her by-the-book cop stopped following the rules she'd set down for their relationship? If Trent's patience ran out and he finally started pursuing her in earnest, how would she be able to resist the security and comfort he offered? Where would she get the strength to turn away from that simmering attraction that had bubbled to the surface tonight?

Katie pushed away to turn off the light and head back to her bedroom. She desperately needed some rest so she could be 100 percent in the morning when she saw Trent again—so she could keep their relationship at the normal she needed. If those anonymous threats didn't break her resolve to remain alone and avoid the temporary security of a relationship that was doomed to fail, Trent Dixon's seductive, unflinching determination would.

Chapter Eight

"Come on, Padre." Trent downed the last of the tepid coffee and set the thermal mug in the console between him and the dog curled up in the passenger seat of his pickup. "Are your muscles getting as stiff as mine?"

Well, *curled up* was a relative term. The moment Trent pulled his attention from the sun rising dimly on the horizon behind Katie's apartment building and spoke to the dog, the former Stinky McPooch leaped to his feet and straddled the center console to rest his neatly trimmed front paws on Trent's thigh. The dog's excited posture and wagging tail diffused the weariness permeating every bone in Trent's body. "You're hungry for some action, aren't you, pal?"

An eager slurp across the scruff of Trent's jaw indicated an affirmative answer. With a laugh, he reached over to attach the new leash to Padre's harness, which peeked through the bright red Kansas City Chiefs sweater he'd gotten to keep the dog warm and to make him an easy target to spot when the mutt dug into the snow he seemed to love so much. "All right, all right, I'm moving."

Padre was in his lap, ready to leap outside into the street, before Trent could turn off the engine he'd been running for the heater and pocket the keys. A slap of cold air and a brisk walk would do him some good, too, after sitting outside Katie's building for most of the night. Olivia Watson and her fiancé, Gabe Knight, had voluntarily ended their date early the evening before to stand watch while Trent went home to shower and try to get some shut-eye. But he'd only lasted a couple hours before coming back to send Liv and Gabe on their way and watch over the Rinaldis himself. There was already more distance than he wanted between him and Katie, and though she was leery of taking any emotional risks and doubtful of her ability to make a relationship work, he had no doubt about what was in his heart. He wasn't going to let any harm come to the woman and child he loved. They were his to protect, even if they never got the chance to become the family he wanted them to be.

"All right, boy." He scratched Padre around the ears and looked into the dog's dark brown eyes, imagining he could talk more sense into him than he'd been able to with Katie last night. "Now mind your manners on the leash. Let's go."

Leading the dog to the sidewalk while he locked up the truck, Trent scanned up and down the block. Although it had been a relatively quiet night, there was plenty of activity this morning, with folks in the neighborhood out shoveling snow or sweeping the blowing flakes off their vehicles and warming up cars as they got ready to head to work or school. He wasn't the only brave soul out walking a pet, either, and there was even one diehard out for a morning jog who'd already worked up enough exertion to mask his face with a cloud of warm breath.

Trent negotiated a silent compromise with Padre by agreeing to walk faster if the dog stopped tugging on the leash. Besides working the kinks from his muscles after sitting in the truck for so long, Trent figured he could kill two birds with one stone, letting the dog manage his business while he scouted the perimeter of Katie's three-story building along with other buildings and patrons of the neighborhood.

While Padre snuffled through the snowdrifts, Trent took note of faces and locations and whether or not anyone was more interested than they should be in anybody else. On the way back, he located the windows to Katie and Tyler's apartment. Behind the curtains and blinds, the lights were on in the rooms he knew to be her bedroom and the kitchen. He slowed his pace when he saw the shadow moving at the kitchen sink and imagined what she might be doing in there. He wondered if she'd gotten any more sleep than he had.

When they'd kissed last night, Katie had given him a little taste of heaven. She'd forgotten the rules, lowered her defenses and clung to him with an abandon that was even hotter and more reality shifting than he'd imagined it would be between them. But then that brain of hers had to kick in. She'd gotten spooked by the possibility of their relationship deepening into something more, and she'd backed off all the way into her violent and unpredictable past. After all this time, Katie still didn't believe in him enough to trust that he'd be there to catch her when she stumbled. He believed in the two of them together enough for the both of them. But she wouldn't let it happen. She blamed herself for screwing up before there was anything between them to destroy.

Okay, so there were a few things about the woman that made him a little crazy—like holding back details after starting a conversation and refusing to explain herself. Like those damn rules, which he supposed were some kind of survival code in her mind. Still, those were just quirks he had to work around; they were challenges he was willing to meet. Trent tried to think of one thing she could do to make him not want her in his life and came up empty. But until she came around to the idea of a relationship, until these threats against her could be stopped, he'd better concentrate on the job at hand. And maybe get back inside the warmth of his truck. "Come on, Padre."

The tan-and-white collie mix trotted along beside him while Trent noted an older woman coming out of Katie's building, trading a friendly nod and a smile with the man who held the door open for her before hurrying in out of the cold. A businessman was backing out of his parking space in the lot while a family was bundling everyone into a minivan. One of the children said something to the mom and she grumbled, fishing her keys out of her pocket and sending him back inside the building to retrieve whatever he'd forgotten. The maintenance super tossed the last of his rock salt on the front steps and pulled the key fob from his retractable key ring to open the door and go in.

Trent glanced up at the kitchen window again. Katie's shadow had moved on to another part of the apartment, leaving him blind to her exact location. Losing track of her for a few seconds shouldn't make him antsy like this. His tired brain needed to tune in to what was off here.

His gaze shot to the front door again. The skin at his nape burned with suspicion. "Ah, hell."

The man who'd held the door for the older woman hadn't used a key fob to enter the building like everyone else. He hadn't needed to.

Trent's breathing deepened, quickened as he glanced around. Everybody else except for the jogger was dressed for the snow-shrouded December morning. But that man…

Brown hair. Long wool coat. *Dress shoes.*

The alarm going off in his head must have traveled down the leash. Padre danced around his legs and woofed.

"Padre, heel." Teaching the dog a new command, he gave a sharp tug on the leash. Padre broke into a run beside him as they made a beeline for the front door. Trent knocked on the window and peered through the glass to see if anyone was inside the lobby. Where had the man gone? "Katie?"

Then he turned to the bank of mailboxes and buzzed her apartment. "Katie? Tyler, you in there?"

When there was no immediate response, he shook the front door handle. He wondered if he could break the lock with a ram of his shoulder, or if he needed to fire a round into it.

"May I help you?" By now he'd gotten someone's attention. The super in the tan coveralls strolled across the lobby, pointing to the no-pets sign on the glass. "I'm sorry, sir. But that dog—"

"KCPD." Trent slapped his badge against the glass and made the startled man read *that* sign. "Open it now. You've got an intruder in there."

"An intruder? But this is a secure—"

"Now!"

"Yes, sir." Jumping at Trent's harsh command, the older man pulled the fob from his belt and swept it over the lock. "Are we in any danger?" he asked, pulling open the door.

"Katie!" Rushing past the super, Trent sprinted up the stairs to the second floor. Padre kept pace, whining with nerves or excitement when Trent skidded to a stop in front of the elevator. Just as he'd feared, the perp had gotten off on the second floor. Katie's floor. A door opened close by and Trent flashed his badge to shoo the curious tenant back into her apartment. "Police, ma'am. Get back inside."

With a quick scan up and down the hallway, Trent saw the rest of the doors were closed or were clicking shut as other curious tenants retreated at the sight of the hulking detective and vocal dog charging down to Katie's door.

"Katie!" His gaze dropped to the nickel-finished door-knob and easily turned it. Ah, hell. He traced his gloved finger over the telltale scratch marks there and on the dead bolt lock higher up, sure signs that both had been tampered with. He glanced up and down that hallway again. One of those closing doors might be hiding a stalker. One instinct said to pursue his suspicion, but another, stronger urge made him flatten his palm and pound on the door. "Katie Lee! Answer me."

"For Pete's sake, Trent, you'll wake the neighbors." The dead bolt turned and she opened the door. Pulling the dog along with him, he pushed her inside and quickly shut the door behind him and locked the dead bolt. "Come in," she muttered sarcastically. "Bring the beast, too. What's a little fine from the tenants' association? Were you the one buzzing to come up?"

"No one came in? No one's here but the two of you? Why didn't you answer?"

"Slow down, Detective."

Her irritation gave way to confusion as he handed the dog's leash off to her and pushed by to make sure every-thing was as it should be. A blue-eyed woman with damp, freshly shampooed tendrils bouncing against her neck was running around in gray slacks and a flannel pajama top, carrying a blouse she was probably getting ready to change into for work. Breakfast on the table. Lunch being packed. "Where's Tyler?"

"In the tub. Why is the dog here? What is going on?"

He went straight to the bathroom door, pulled off his watch cap and leaned his ear against the wood, relieved to hear the sounds of a little boy playing with ships in the water on the other side. He checked both bedrooms and the hall closet before rejoining Katie in the main room. "Someone tried to break in."

"Inside the building?"

"At your front door. I must have scared him off." Her knuckles turned white around the dog's leash. He should be outside, checking for signs of the intruder's escape route, making sure he wasn't still lurking in the building. But he couldn't leave Katie unprotected, not until he understood what the hell was going on and had a plan to deal with it. "He'd gotten your knob unlocked. Fortunately, you had the dead bolt in place. You didn't hear anything?"

"No. I was running a bath for Tyler."

Speaking of, a barefoot boy in superhero underpants ran out of the bathroom. "Padre!"

"Tyler," Katie cautioned, "where are your clothes?"

"Mom, Padre came to see me." Dropping to his knees, he hugged his arms around the dog's neck. There was licking and giggling and tail wagging and petting before Tyler jumped to his feet and the dog bounded after him. "Come on, boy. Let's eat."

Tyler paused to give Trent a quick hug around his hips, then ran back to follow the dog as Padre sniffed his way around the apartment. The little boy stopped at the table to scoop up a forkful of scrambled eggs and stuff it into his mouth. Then he stabbed another bite and dropped it to the floor, where the skinny dog gobbled it up.

"Tyler," Katie chided. "Not at the table." She hurried to the kitchen window, where Trent was pulling open the blinds to check outside. Where had that guy disappeared to? If he was still inside, Trent would have to do a room-to-room search, and with eighteen apartments in this building, the guy could stay one step ahead of him, sneaking out while he cleared each space. If he'd already made his escape… "Padre can't be in here. Tyler, you need to finish dressing before you catch a cold." She latched on to Trent's sleeve when he brushed past her to get another view from her bedroom window. "This isn't a friendly visit for Tyler's sake, is it? What's going on?" When she peeked out the window behind him, her tone changed from suspiciously annoyed to simply suspicious. "Who are you looking for?"

Trent looked over the top of her head to see a blur of movement. Son of a… The alarm in his blood reengaged. He caught Katie by the shoulders and turned her attention to the man in a long coat stumbling through the snow. "Him, Katie. Do you recognize him?"

Trent was already backing toward the door as she shook her head and faced him. "Who's that? Why is he running?"

"I intend to find out." Trent pulled open the apartment door. "Lock up behind me. No one comes in except me."

"Trent—"

"Lock it, Katie!"

He had to get to that pervert before he reached whatever vehicle he was headed for. Once he heard the secure click of the dead bolt sliding into place, Trent booked it into overtime, running down the stairs, skipping a few with each stride. He shoved open the outside door and rushed straight across the snowy ground. "Police! Stop!"

The man with the dress shoes might have cold feet, but he was fast. He dashed across the street and climbed into a black sports car. He had the engine revving before Trent reached the pavement. What the hell? Who was this guy? What did he want with Katie?

Trent held up his badge and pulled his gun. "Police! Get out of the car!"

But the perp showed no signs of cooperating. He jerked his wheels to the left and floored it.

Trent planted his feet and took aim as the driver swerved out of his parking stall. "Stop! Or I'll shoot!"

He squinted and turned his face from the pelting of slush and ice crystals. The car roared down the street, and by the time Trent could look back and get a bead on the fishtailing back tires, he realized he didn't have a clear shot. There were too many people around, frozen in their morning routines, some ducking behind their vehicles, others standing in open ground, staring at him— including the curvy brunette with her face pressed to the second-story window.

"Son of a…" His breath whooshed out on a frustrated curse as the car veered around the corner and sped away. There wasn't even time to get to his truck and get turned around to pursue the suspect.

But he wasn't about to give up on finding the answers he needed and putting a stop to the danger escalating around Katie and Tyler. With a wave of reassurance to the people around him, Trent holstered his weapon and pulled out his phone.

Max's gruff voice answered. "It's early, junior, and I'm in bed with my wife. This better be good."

"Apologies to Rosie. I need you to run a plate for me."

The tenor of Max's tone changed instantly and Trent imagined his partner rolling out of bed with an urgency belying his burly stature. "You need backup? Everything okay?"

"No. But I'm not sure what I'm dealing with yet." He strode back up the sidewalk "A guy just tried to pick the lock on Katie's apartment. He drove off after I chased him from the building."

"Hell, I'd run, too, if I had a defensive tackle chasing me down," Max teased, writing down the number Trent gave him.

His partner didn't even question that he was at Katie's this early in the morning. "The perp matched the general description of the guy taking pictures at the theater last night. I want to know why he was here."

"I'm on it. You stay with her. I'll call as soon as I know anything." He heard Max exchanging a kiss and muttering some kind of explanation to his wife. "Anything else?"

"Just get me the info, Max."

"Will do."

"Thanks, brother."

Katie was waiting for him when he knocked on her door. Trent pushed inside and locked it behind him. Baggy plaid flannel draping over those generous breasts shouldn't trigger this instant desire in him, but he'd had a lot of practice ignoring those traitorous impulses around Katie. It was harder, though, to ignore the concern in those wide blue eyes, or to turn away from the wary frown that dimpled her forehead. Trent pulled off his glove and brushed her hair away from her worried expression. He'd barely felt a sample of her warm, velvety skin before she pulled away from his touch.

"Did you catch him?" she whispered, darting her eyes toward Tyler and Padre playing on the floor beside the Christmas tree.

Right. The rules. Although Trent wanted nothing more than to take her in his arms and feel with his own two hands that she was safe, she was in touch-me-not mode this morning. He shook his head and unzipped his coat before crossing to check the lock on the kitchen window. "I got the plate number on his car, so hopefully it'll be enough to ID this guy."

He peered outside to see the sun glinting off the snow and the world turning back to normal before heading through the apartment to ensure that all the access points were secure. A parade of mom, dog and boy followed him through the apartment.

"How did he get in?" Katie asked.

"It's not that hard if you bide your time and have a charming smile."

"He conned his way in here?" She snapped her fingers and shooed Tyler and Padre across the hall when they reached her bedroom. "Clothes. Now, young man." Departing on a three-toned sigh, Tyler grabbed Padre's collar and went into his room. Once she was certain her son was changing for school, Katie tugged on the sleeve of Trent's coat and pulled him into her bedroom. "You're going to scare Tyler if you keep this up."

The fresh, flowery scent that was all Katie was stronger in here. But he conquered the urge to draw in a deep, savoring breath and crossed to the curtains to secure the window and fire escape outside. "The dog will distract him."

"Not entirely. He's a sensitive kid." He shivered at the touch of her fingers at the nape of his neck. But what he'd mistaken for a caress was pure practicality. She held up a palmful of road slush that was melting on his collar, then carried it over to the damp towel tossed across the bed from her morning shower to wipe her hand. "My God, you're a cold mess. You were out there all night, weren't you?"

"Most of it."

"I thought I saw your truck. I couldn't sleep, either, after our...discussion." She reached up and used the towel to dab at the moisture still beading on his neck and jaw. Ah, hell. Now, *that* was a caress. Goose bumps prickled across his skin in the wake of her touch, and her soft sigh teased something deeper inside. But she must have realized she'd crossed the very boundary she'd asked him to respect and quickly pulled away to stuff the towel into the hamper in her closet. Her shoulders came back with a forced resolve and she crossed to the desk she used as a home office. She picked up a stack of papers from the printer there.

"So I did some work, too. I compiled a list of Leland Asher's known associates and ran them through my database to see if there were any hits that matched up. I've been doing it backward—lining up the cases and then looking for connections between them to pop. This time I plugged in a bunch of suspect names we've been tossing around and ran them through the cold case data."

Fine. They were safe for now. He couldn't do a damn thing until he heard back from Max. So he let her turn the conversation to work. "Did you find anything?"

Katie nodded and handed him the papers. "Isabel Asher—Leland's sister—was a sorority sister of Beverly Eisenbach's at, get this, Williams College."

He thumbed through the stack. "The place where you and Tyler are doing the play?"

She pointed to the grainy printout from a twenty-five-year-old college annual. "The blonde in the front row is Isabel. Dr. Eisenbach is on the far left."

"Eisenbach's the shrink who counseled Matt Asher and Stephen March as teens?" He recognized the younger images of the two women who'd each held a spot on the person of interest board at the squad's team meeting earlier in the week. "You think that's how Dr. Eisenbach and Leland met? Through Isabel?"

"You'd have to ask Bev Eisenbach to find that out." She pointed to the date at the bottom of the photo. "But there's a reasonable chance that she knew the Asher family years before she counseled Leland's nephew. This is dated before he was even born. Maybe she's more than Leland's latest girlfriend. Having the previous acquaintance could be the reason he selected her to counsel his nephew, Matt. But if they've known each other since they were in their twenties, isn't it possible that their relationship has gone on for a lot longer than we realized? Maybe she counseled Leland for some reason—grief, stress, dealing with his sister's addiction? She might have confidential information on him that we could use in our investigation. Maybe he even confessed to some of his crimes, or the hits we suspect he paid for. Dr. Eisenbach's practice is one of the offices I've sent requests to for information. They confirmed that Matt Asher and Stephen March were former patients, but any requests for a complete patient list have been ignored."

"This is good stuff, sunshine. Maybe even enough to ask the lieutenant for a warrant to get a look at Eisenbach's records." Trent looked at another picture, this time of a young man with long blond hair or a blond wig, dressed in a Shakespearean costume. "What's this?" The actor's dark, beady eyes looked familiar. "Is this the Grim Reaper?"

Katie hugged her arms in front of her, clearly feeling a little less comfortable with this piece of information. "Francis Sergel about twenty-five years ago. I found him through my facial recognition software."

Trent squinted the name beneath the theater program picture into focus. "Frank Reinhardt?"

"Sergel must be a stage name he adopted. Looks like he's playing Hamlet."

Trent couldn't imagine that walking, talking skeleton of a man playing anything heroic. "He has ties to Asher?"

"Lieutenant Rafferty-Taylor didn't ask me to pursue him as a suspect, so I didn't exactly have permission to dig through criminal records. But after the last few nights at the theater, I wanted to know if I should be worried about him."

Was that what had her squirming inside her own skin— that she'd broken a procedure rule? "I'll request it."

She offered up a wan smile. "Thanks."

"Not a problem. I didn't like Sergel or that Doug Price, either. I want to make sure they check out." He flipped to the next page and skimmed the information. "So Sergel, er, Reinhardt, has a record?"

"Minor stuff. Nothing violent. Possession of narcotics. A DUI. He never went to prison. It was all time served and community service. And court-ordered NA meetings."

"Like Stephen March." And Isabel Asher. And any of a number of pushers and addicts who'd worked for and bought from and crossed paths with Asher's criminal empire.

"A decade earlier, but yes." She sank onto the edge of her bed as if her legs had grown too weak to hold her. She'd made the same realization he had. The team's idea of a *Strangers on a Train* setup behind several of their unsolved crimes could no longer be discounted as a mere theory. "It's a small world, isn't it?"

Trent knelt on the carpet in front of her, relieved to see that she didn't swat away a comforting touch when he rested his hand on her knee. "Cold cases are built on circumstantial evidence more than anything else. There are an awful lot of circumstances that your research has linked together. Now we just have to prove that Leland Asher is behind it all."

Her gaze met his and she tried to smile. "Good luck with that."

"Look, I'm going to take this information and run with it. I'll get Sergel and Price and Dr. Eisenbach and maybe even Leland himself all in for interviews. We'll get the doctor's patient list and see if she counseled Leland. We'll make a case against Asher and put him back in prison where he belongs." He stroked his fingers over the gray wool of her slacks. "But my immediate concern is those threats you've been getting. I've got a call in to Max to see if he can run down the name of that guy who got away. You didn't recognize him, did you?"

"From the back? Running away?"

"He was wearing dress shoes instead of snow boots. Like the photographer you saw at the theater."

The telephone on her bedside table rang and she jumped. Trent squeezed her knee before standing up and giving her the space to move around the bed and answer it. "So that's why he looked at my driver's license."

"If it's the same guy who defaced your laptop, yeah. It'd be easy to find you." Trent caught her by the hand before she left him entirely. "I don't suppose I could talk you into packing a bag for you and Tyler and moving in with me until this all blows over? It's hell sleeping in my truck, and your couch isn't big enough."

He needed her to read between the lines of his teasing tone and understand he was drop-dead serious. *I'm not going anywhere and I'm not leaving you alone.*

Her fingers trembled for a moment inside his grasp before she pulled away and picked up the cordless receiver from its cradle. "Hello? Yes?" Trent watched the color drain from her face. "Who is this? Why are you doing this to me?"

"Katie?"

She punched the button to put the call on speakerphone and held the receiver between them as an electronically altered voice filled the room. "—want to hurt you, Katie Lee. But you've left me no choice. I know what scares you. The dark. A syringe. Your murdering father. Losing your child."

Trent dropped the photos Katie had printed out and grabbed the phone from her hand. "This is the police. Who is this?"

He gritted his teeth at the answering laugh. "You were warned. Even your boyfriend's not going to be able to save you now."

The click of the disconnecting call echoed across the room. Trent hung up her phone and pulled his from his coat. He'd call Max again to find out who'd just dialed her number. Although he'd bet good money this wraith stalking Katie had used an untraceable cell.

Katie sank to her knees, crawling across the carpet to pick up the photos. "He's not going to hurt you, sunshine. I won't let him." His partner picked up. "Max?"

But Katie was more focused on some distant point

inside her head than in any kind of shock. She sat back on her heels and crumpled the papers in her fist. "It's these."

"Pictures? Printouts? The mess I made?" After relaying the message to Max, Trent picked up the rest of the papers and tried to understand the wheels turning in her head. "You're not talking to me, woman. What do you mean?"

She blinked and brought those cornflower-blue eyes into focus on him. "It's the research I'm doing on these cold case files." She braced her hand on his shoulder to stand and hurried to her computer. Trent followed, anxious to catch up on her train of thought. "I've opened up the wrong can of worms somewhere—I've breached some piece of information I shouldn't have. That's what he wants me to stop."

Trent looked over her shoulder as she booted up her computer, plugged in her portable hard drive and turned on the hot-spot security device. "The brass isn't about to stop a criminal investigation. Even if the lieutenant takes you off the case and reassigns you, we'll still be going after Asher. Are you sure?"

"Every time I ping another database, every time I send an email request—that's when he contacts me." With the equipment in place, she tucked her hair behind her ears and went to work. "I need to run a full system diagnostic. It may be on my computer at work, too. He's mirroring me."

"What does that mean?"

"Somebody's tapped into my computer. Or maybe the portable hard drive. Even if he's not copying my data, he can see what sites I go to. He's been tracking every movement I make online."

"How can you tell?"

She'd gotten into the belly of the programming now

and was scrolling through code. "Every time I get a little more information about Leland Asher, every time I discover another piece of the puzzle that can build our case against him, something happens. That man at the theater. Vandalizing my laptop. He's tracking me somehow. Either visually or online."

Stop what you're doing, the message had said. "They want you to stop investigating Leland Asher?"

She pointed to the gibberish on the screen. "It's all right here. But I've been too distracted to see it. It's a virus, a replicating virus that copies everything I do to another computer. Someone got close enough to my laptop or portable hard drive to plant it."

"At the theater? There's too much security at HQ."

"I don't know. I may be able to track down the source." Her fingers were flying over the keyboard, clicking on icons and typing in commands he didn't understand. "I need to notify tech support at work to sweep the systems, just in case they've found a back door into the KCPD network. But there are enough safeguards that that might be difficult, even for an experienced hacker. More likely, it's my personal account that's been..."

She picked up the hot-spot device and turned it over. "Do you have your pocketknife?"

Trent reached into the pocket of his jeans to retrieve the knife. He marveled at the woman's intelligence as she pried open the device. "Katie?"

She dropped the pieces onto the desk and sank back in her chair. Trent didn't have to be a genius like her to see that the innards weren't connected, so it hadn't blocked any intrusive signals. She could have been hacked almost anywhere if that wasn't working—at the coffee shop, at the theater, at home.

He pried the open knife from her grip. "Where did you buy that thing? Who would have access to disable it besides you?"

"Anybody. I bought it months ago. I keep it in my bag. If they could get to my laptop, they could get to the hot-spot device. Then I'd be as vulnerable as if I had no security on my computer components at all. I am so going to lose my job over this, aren't I?" She closed her hands into fists. "Such a screwup."

"You're not," he insisted. He dropped down on one knee beside her and captured her jaw between his thumb and fingers to turn her gaze toward his. "This just means there's somebody who thinks he's as smart as you out there. He's a lot more calculating and doesn't give a damn about who he hurts." He tightened his grasp and pulled her forward to meet his kiss. Katie's lips were full and sweet and shyly responsive in a way that shattered the caution around his heart and kindled a fire in his blood. "I believe in you, sunshine. Maybe this is a break in the investigation, an opportunity to trace it back to some hacker with ties to Asher. Now take a deep breath and figure this out."

Her hands came up to cup his face and she smiled. "I don't know why you're so good to me."

"That's easy." He leaned in to kiss that worry dimple on her forehead. "Because I lo—"

"Wait a minute." Trent reeled in the ill-timed confession as a new idea reenergized her. He folded the knife blade and returned it to the safety of his jeans pocket while Katie went back to her keyboard. "I should be able to track back to the date the device was disabled. The time should help us zero in on a location and who could have—"

She drew back with a gasp, her hands raised as row after row of words scrolled across her computer. After the first line, they were the same words, repeating over and over and over until they filled the screen.

Stop, Katie.
Die, Katie.
Die, Katie.
Die, Katie.
Die, Katie.
Die, Katie.

"Trent?"

"Son of a bitch." Trent pulled her to her feet. He wanted to smash the monitor to erase the threats she'd somehow triggered. He would have ripped the whole thing out of the wall and tossed it across the room if some little sane part of his brain hadn't remembered he was a cop, looking at a desk full of key evidence. "Log out of there. Do something. Fast."

Katie quickly shut down her Wi-Fi connection and pulled the cable connecting her router to the internet. He turned off the screen himself before she backed into him. His arms instantly went around her. "Easy, sunshine. You're okay."

She shook her head, the nylon of his coat rustling against her hair. "Why is this happening to me? I'm just one little cog on the team. I'm background. I'm nobody. We're all trying to solve cold cases and connect them to Leland Asher. All I do is the research. Why was that man here? Why is he trying to scare me?"

Probably because they were getting closer to the truth, closer to making a major case against Asher stick. And someone in Asher's camp was targeting Katie because she was the weakest link on the team—she hadn't had police training and she didn't carry a gun, but she was vital to proving that there was nothing alleged about the mob boss and his illegal activities. "Their time to shut us down is running out. Asher gets released from prison today."

She shook within his grasp. He knew the moment she decided she needed him more than she needed the distance between them. Turning in his arms, Katie shoved open the front of his coat and burrowed against his chest. Her fingers clenched in the layers of his shi███ the skin and muscle underneath. Trent threaded ████ers through her damp waves and cradled the back of her head, dropping his lips to the fragrant sunshine of her hair, holding her tightly against his strength.

"Mom? Are you okay?" a soft voice whispered from the open doorway. Despite the grip he had on Padre's collar, Tyler's eyes were wide with concern. Smart kid. He could see his mother was scared.

He just prayed the boy couldn't see that Trent was more than a little frightened for Katie, too.

"I'm okay, sweetie," Katie answered, her voice strong to reassure her son. "I just got some bad news." She tried to push away, but Trent wasn't budging.

Instead, he held his hand out to the little boy. "You're going to come stay at my house for a couple days, buddy. Okay?"

With a nod that didn't quite erase his frown, Tyler left the dog and ran across the room to hug Katie. She lifted her son into her arms and Trent wrapped them both in his shielding embrace.

Chapter Nine

Trent sat at his desk, staring at the twelve pictures on his computer. Six victims, six suspects. Plenty of circumstantial evidence to link one to another, but no real proof as to who was ultimately behind either the unsolved murders or the threats against Katie. But the key to solving the crimes attributed to Leland Asher and his criminal network had to be staring him in the face. If only he could get those pictures to talk.

That one of the police department's information technologists was being stalked and receiving threats promising to kill her or harm her son if she didn't stop poking around with her research meant the team had gotten too close to uncovering some long-buried truths. Their cold case investigation was heating up.

Maybe more than Trent wanted.

Not for the first time that day, his gaze wandered across the maze of detectives' desks to the cubicle where Katie sat, surrounded by a desktop computer, a stack of print files and a tall cup of some mocha-latte thing. She wore a pencil in her hair and a hands-free headset to talk on the phone with other tech gurus assigned to the department. The threats that had frightened her at home only seemed to motivate her now. Maybe diving into work was a way to distract herself from the fears for her and Tyler's safety. Or possibly, skipping lunch and never leaving her computer was some kind of atonement for allowing an outsider to breach her computers and gain inside information on the cold case squad's progress on different investigations. Or maybe there was still a little bit of that teenage girl who charged into battle left inside her, and instead of cowing her into submission, the danger that had come to her very doorstep had inspired her to take action—to save the investigation, to find justice for those victims whose murders had yet to be solved, to save her son.

Although Trent didn't understand all the jargon, Katie and the tech team at the lab had scoured all her computers, and, as she suspected, the mirroring had been done through the hot-spot device on her laptop and portable hard drive. The KCPD network was secure and only the public-record files she'd been using in her database had been accessed. Her laptop was back from the lab—unfortunately, with no usable prints but her own and his. And, with a legal warrant and approval from Ginny Rafferty-Taylor, Katie was back at work again, doing a little hacking herself to find out when the virus had been planted so she could determine her location at that time and identify anyone who might have had access to plant the bug in her system.

A paper wad smacked Trent in the forehead, drawing his attention back to the desk across from his. "Really?"

"Hey, I didn't want to be the only one working." Max Krolikowski had plenty of ammunition on his messy desk, but he pointed to the stray missile that had landed on the tidy expanse of Trent's blotter before hanging up his phone. "That's the number that called Katie this morning." Trent unfolded the note and smoothed it open to read the information Max had jotted there. "Just like you suspected. Disposable cell. It's been turned off so there's no way to trace it."

Trent slipped the paper into a folder and glanced down at the license plate number and name of the rental company that had leased the black sports car to a John Smith, aka Mr. Fancy Dress Shoes, aka he still didn't have any freaking ID on the guy who'd gotten far too close to Katie and Tyler that morning. Just a bunch more puzzle pieces and no big picture yet.

"However, it does belong to a type of phone sold exclusively at your favorite big-box discount department store over the past year."

Trent sat back in his chair. Like the anonymous John Smith with the fake license and credit card, that was almost worse than no help. "There are a dozen of those stores in the city. Assuming the perp bought it in KC."

"Yeah, but they all have surveillance cameras in their electronics departments."

"Are you willing to sit through twelve months of surveillance footage from all those stores to see who bought a phone and then try to identify John Smith or anybody else who's come up in one of our cases?"

"It's a long shot."

"It's worse than a long shot."

"But I'd do it for Katie."

Trent agreed. "So would I."

With an answering nod, Max picked up his phone again. "I'll start calling, see if the stores even keep security footage from that far back."

"I'll find out if this guy used his John Smith ID to buy the phone or anything else."

Trent closed out the pictures on his computer screen

but paused before picking up his own phone to help Max with one of the tedious, but necessary, demands of police work. "What's the point of threatening Katie? She's not going to be arresting anybody. This bastard should be coming after me or you or Liv and Jim, or anybody else on the team, if he wanted to misdirect us or slow down our investigation."

His partner hung up the phone without dialing. "You think this Smith dude tried to break in to her apartment to harm her? Not just to steal her computer or something like that?"

"I didn't give him a chance to finish the job. And he wasn't inclined to stop for a chat."

Max scrubbed his fingers over his jaw in a thoughtful sigh. "Are the threats affecting her work?"

Trent glanced over to see Katie riffling through the files on her desk before tapping her headset and answering whatever the party on the other end of the call had asked. "She seems as scatterbrained and brilliant as ever."

"Interesting." If Max meant something by that cryptic response, he didn't elaborate. "But the scaring part's working?"

Trent could still feel the marks on his skin where she'd finally turned to him for solace and held on to him until her trembling had stopped. And he'd never forget the worry stamped on Tyler's sweet, innocent face. "It's even getting to her son. I mean, Jim's at the school shadowing Tyler during the day, so we know he's safe for now. But how do I reassure a nine-year-old that everything's going to be okay if I don't even know what I'm up against?"

"I don't have kids— Hell, that's a scary thought, ain't it—me and kids?" Max propped his elbows on his desk and steepled his fingers together. "But I think you just need to be there for them."

"That's what Katie needs, too." Trent summoned half a grin, appreciating Max's attempt at deep philosophical advice. "But I won't lie. It's hard to be spending that much time with her, given our history."

"It's hard because you're a good guy. You think things through. You wait for an invitation. You don't just haul off and kiss a woman like I did Rosie when we first met and I was toasted out of my..." Max slapped his palm on top of his desk. "Well, hell's bells, junior, you *did* kiss her. And not one of those Dudley Do-Right pecks on the cheek, either, I'll bet."

Groaning, Trent tried to temper Max's stunned excitement. "They were a mistake."

"They? More than once?" Max swore under his breath. "You've been holding out on me. About time it happened between you two."

Trent glared at his partner. "Nothing happened."

"No fireworks?" Max looked disappointed. Oh, yeah, there'd been plenty of spontaneous combustion between them on that kitchen stool. But the *Die, Katie* bombardment on her computer screen had reminded Trent that Katie needed his protection, not his love. Max leaned forward and whispered, "Wrong kind of fireworks?"

Give his love life a rest, already. "It's Christmas, not Independence Day."

"Huh?"

"Wrong time for fireworks. I was taking advantage of a vulnerable moment." Of several vulnerable moments, it would seem.

Max grumbled a curse and sorted through the scattered papers on his desk. "Junior, you don't know how to take advantage. If Katie wasn't willing, you wouldn't—"

"Tyler's safety is her priority." Trent pulled a phone book from a desk drawer and started looking up numbers, as relieved to be ending the conversation and getting back to work as he'd been to air some of his concerns with his most trusted friend in the first place. "And it should be. It's my priority, too. I want to find out who this jackass is and put him in my interrogation room. I want to get him out of their lives so Tyler can just be a kid again and Katie can…"

What? Go back to being his buddy when he wanted to be her bedmate? Her soul mate? Her everything? Now that she and Tyler were staying with him, his worries about their safety had eased a fraction, but remembering not to push for everything he wanted from her grew harder with every passing minute.

"Earth to big guy." Olivia knocked on the corner of Trent's desk, pulling him from his thoughts. "The lieutenant wants us in her office. The press is covering Leland Asher's release."

Setting aside his troubling thoughts, Trent pushed to his feet, taking a moment to tuck in his corduroy shirt and the thermal Henley he wore underneath before following Liv and Max across the room. Katie ended her call and scooped up her laptop, darting into the office on a waft of flowery scent that reminded Trent of freshly shampooed hair and warm curves pressed against his body. Wisely avoiding broadcasting that woman's physical effect on him, he took a position standing at the back of the room while Katie set up her laptop and sat at the front of the group. When his gaze locked on to a sly glimpse of cornflower blue directed back at him, Trent wondered if Katie was making a point of keeping her distance, too.

"Let's see what our friend has to say." Lieutenant Rafferty-Taylor turned up the sound on the television screen as a twinkling of camera flashes captured the image of Leland Asher walking through the prison exit into the bright, cold sunshine of the wintry afternoon.

Looking like a politician on a campaign stump, Asher waved to the crowd of eager reporters, curiosity seekers and armed guards who were there to make sure nothing got out of hand before the alleged mobster left the premises. Although the once stocky man had lost a lot of weight, probably due to the cancer, there was a sense of entitlement to his carriage. Plus, he wore the impeccably tailored suit and dress coat of a man who still had access to plenty of money. The man with a briefcase beside him led the way to a small podium, where he identified himself as Asher's attorney and made a statement regarding his client's release.

But the words coming from the television were just white noise as Katie began to fidget in her chair. She drummed her fingers over her keyboard without typing anything and kept drawing her hair between her fists in a ponytail before letting it fall back to her shoulders when she realized she had no clip to secure it. What was buzzing through that brain of hers now?

An elbow butted up against his, diverting Trent's attention to his far too observant partner. "You up for this, junior? You want me to take over shadowing Katie?"

"No." He wasn't about to leave Tyler and Katie's security up to anyone else. "I want you to be there to take up the slack in case I can't get the job done."

"You not get a job done? Trust me, junior. That'll never happen."

Olivia sat on the corner of the table. She nodded to the TV. "He's on. Turn it up."

A dark-haired woman wearing a fur coat ran up to the podium to kiss Leland's cheek. The woman had a striking strand of white framing her face when she turned to the camera. And while she looked adoringly up at the gaunt, graying man, he wound his arm around her waist and held her to his side.

Katie pointed to the screen. "That's Beverly Eisenbach, Mr. Asher's significant other. She's the psychologist who counseled Matt Asher and Stephen March as teenagers."

"Any response to your query about whether or not Leland was ever a patient of hers?" the lieutenant asked.

Katie shrugged. "Talk to her attorney and get a warrant?"

Trent tuned out Asher's pontification about learning from his mistakes and how his incarceration hadn't affected his business investments one iota, as well as the updates on his health. Taking Lieutenant Rafferty-Taylor's lead, he turned the gathering into an impromptu staff meeting. "I tracked down the house mother from the sorority Bev Eisenbach and Isabel Asher belonged to. She's retired now, but she remembers the two of them taking classes and hanging out together before Isabel left school. Night and day, she called them. It wasn't just a blonde-brunette thing, either. The house mother said she never understood how two young women with such different personalities got along so well. Dr. Eisenbach was neat, organized, intent on keeping her scholarships and earning her degree, while Isabel was more of a free spirit who was there for the social opportunities."

The petite blonde who led the cold case group folded her arms in front of her and nodded, urging Trent to continue. "Does the house mother remember meeting Leland? Can we prove that Leland and Dr. Eisenbach knew each other twenty-five years ago? And does that information do anything to help our case?"

"The house mother remembers Leland coming on campus to attend events with Isabel. They had no parents, so he was more than a big brother to her."

Olivia chimed in. "We can trace suspected criminal activity to Leland all the way back to that time. He was already starting to amass his fortune, so I'm sure Bev would have been interested in meeting Isabel's big brother."

"Maybe that's what she liked about Isabel," Max interjected. "She could hook her up to a man who was destined to make a lot of money. Clearly, it paid off for her."

Trent thrust his fingers into the back pockets of his jeans. "The house mother remembers the guy Isabel Asher was dating, too. 'A prissy Italian guy' is how she described him."

"Francisco Dona." Katie supplied the name as she typed on her laptop and read the info off the screen. "He was a small-time dealer and user. Looks like they dated each other, or at least used together, on and off for several years until she died. He was questioned as a suspect in Isabel's death, but no charges were ever filed."

Trent picked up on a small detail. "You said *was*. He died in a motorcycle accident. Did anyone ever investigate his death as a possible homicide?"

Katie shook her head. "ME's report said he died of head trauma. He suspected Dona was under the influence. He found a trace amount of drugs in his system."

"But Mr. Dona passed about a month after Isabel's overdose," the lieutenant confirmed.

"There's nothing suspicious about the timing of that," Max groused with sarcasm. "Can anyone say retaliation?"

Trent agreed. "If Leland and Isabel were as close as the house mother claims, then it makes sense that he'd order a hit on Dona. It wouldn't be the first time an accident was staged to cover up a murder."

Katie continued to read the information on her computer. "Even if Francisco Dona didn't provide Isabel with the drugs that killed her, Asher could have still blamed him. According to this, there were no signs of anyone trying to revive Isabel after she collapsed. There wasn't even a 9-1-1 call until her son, Matt, discovered the body."

Even though they were talking about alleged criminals, Katie's voice trailed away in sympathy. She knew firsthand what it was like to deal with the death of a parent, and might even be remembering her own mother's murder. Trent pushed away from the wall where he was leaning, wanting to go to her. But the sharp blue gaze darting his way was a warning to keep his distance. Either she was telling him she could handle this or she was asking him to keep the complications of the relationship growing between them private.

"Great." Liv's sarcasm matched Max's. "Another murder we'd like to attribute to Asher that we can't prove. How does this guy keep getting away with it?" She turned to Katie. "Can we at least talk with the ME who wrote the report?"

"That would be Dr. Carson." Katie turned her focus back to her computer and pulled up the name on the report before shaking her head. "He retired with early-onset Alzheimer's a couple of years ago. Your brother Niall replaced him."

Liv groaned at the latest twist. "Does anybody else think that if we could just shuffle all these players in the right order that we'd solve a half dozen murders and put Asher away for good?"

Trent and Max and Katie all raised their hands and Olivia laughed before Lieutenant Rafferty-Taylor directed their attention back to the television. "He's leaving."

Hand in hand, Leland Asher and Bev Eisenbach walked to a waiting limousine, where another group was waiting for him. Trent recognized Asher's longtime chauffeur and bodyguard and spotted a couple more thugs watching the audience like Secret Service men. A young man with glasses—Leland's nephew, Matt—climbed out of the long black car and extended his arm. The two generations shook hands before Leland pulled his nephew in for a showy hug and whispered something in his ear.

Trent couldn't be certain, but had Matt Asher arched his brows over the rim of his glasses and made eye contact with Bev Eisenbach before the hug ended? Or was he alerting the group to the fans with more questions and accusations surging their way?

Either way, Leland remained coolly unperturbed by the rush of attention and turned at the people calling his name.

"One last question, Mr. Asher." A television reporter with long, dark hair thrust her microphone in his face. "How do you feel?"

"Like a free man." Leland laughed and pulled up his pant leg to show off the parole bracelet on his ankle. "Except for the new jewelry the state has so graciously given me."

He waved aside the follow-up questions and ushered

Bev into the limo before he and Matt and the bodyguard climbed in behind her. The network camera panned the crowd, getting shots of protesters and supporters alike, people who thought, like the cold case squad, that Asher had gotten away with murder, and others—friendly plants, perhaps—who waved signs and shouted about "freeing the innocent."

When the camera scanned back to the limousine driving away, a far too familiar image near the back of the crowd shot adrenaline into Trent's bloodstream. In three strides, he was across the office, tapping at the screen. "Are we recording this? Can we get a recording?"

Katie turned her laptop around and typed. "I can get a feed off the station's website. Wait…"

"What is it, junior?" Max asked.

She pulled up the website as they gathered around her. "I've got it. They're replaying the interview."

"Freeze it. There." Trent rested a hand on her shoulder and pointed to the man in the crowd who'd just snapped a photograph of the group at the limousine. Brown hair, long wool coat. Although he couldn't see the telltale shoes, he recognized the nondescript features and receding hairline. "That's John Smith. That's the guy who tried to break in to Katie's apartment."

"Is he part of Asher's entourage?" the lieutenant asked.

"Is he a reporter?" was Liv's guess.

"Hold on." Katie went for a more definitive answer. Using her mouse, she framed the suspect in the picture and clicked a screen shot of his image. "Now that we've got a face, I can blow it up and run him through recognition protocols. If he's in the system, I can track him down."

She pulled back when a private investigator's license

showed up on the screen, along with three different driver's licenses and a state ID card. John Smith apparently had several aliases he used, and not a one of them looked legit lined up like that. But there was at least one thing in common on two of the cards—an address.

Trent pulled his notepad and jotted it down. "That's downtown. Probably an office building."

Katie looked up at Trent. "Go get him."

Chapter Ten

Katie glanced over for the umpteenth time at her flowered bag sitting in the corner of the greenroom backstage, making sure no one had opened it to mess with the contents inside. Good. Still latched. Still safe.

Her research had indicated that her device had been hacked almost two weeks earlier. That day she'd taken Tyler to school, stopped by the coffee shop, gone to work, and hadn't left until it was time to pick up Tyler at his after-school club and go straight to rehearsal. And since she wouldn't count her son as a suspect, and no one at work had any reason to track her research since they could access the same info themselves, that left someone at the coffee shop or here at the show to have tampered with her hot-spot device.

Her money was on someone involved with the play—or who could hide out at the theater undetected. So her suspicions of everyone here were riding high. But since she was alone for the moment while Doug and the cast were onstage going over last-minute notes before tomorrow's final dress rehearsal, she figured it was safe to let the messenger bag out of her sight for the few seconds it would take her to hang up the costumes she was ironing in the women's dressing room.

She set the iron on its end and gathered up the long dresses she'd prepped for the last run-through before opening night and carried them into the women's dressing room. She could hear Doug Price's voice booming through the auditorium and was glad that Trent was in there with Tyler, maybe trading a wink or a thumbs-up to let her son know that Doug's dramatic speech about "moments" and bringing the audience to tears meant the temperamental director was pleased with the way the show had come together. She was doubly glad that Trent was there to keep an eye on Tyler, to make sure her son had nothing to worry about except remembering his lines and making his entrances.

Because they weren't safe. Not yet. The threat was still out there.

When Trent and Max had gone to John Smith's downtown address that afternoon, they'd found a ransacked office, a few drops of blood that indicated there'd been an altercation of some kind and no sign of Smith. A BOLO on the rental car hadn't turned it up yet, either. That meant Smith, whoever he really was, was still out there, still watching, still looking for a way to get to her. Whether he was a spy for Leland Asher or someone with a more personal interest in her, she felt less and less that keeping Trent at arm's length was a good idea. The only time she'd felt safe since finding that message scribbled in the snow, the only time that Tyler acted like a normal kid, was when Detective Dixon was around.

Katie caught a glimpse of her pale features in the bright lights of the dressing room mirrors and cringed. No wonder Tyler was scared for her. Sleep had been a rare commodity the past few days. She touched the shadows beneath her eyes and wished she had Trent's arms around her right now, so she could soak up the comfort of his warmth, be reenergized by the thrill of his possessive kiss and feel secure enough to drop her guard for a few moments and simply take a normal breath without looking over her shoulder or second-guessing every move she made and worrying about Tyler.

With the gun and badge on his belt, and the sheer size of those shoulders and chest, Trent didn't exactly fit the role of backstage parent. But he'd made it clear that until he could arrest John Smith and prove that the part-time private investigator/full-time con man was the person who'd threatened her, Trent was going to be spending a whole lot of time with her. His days, at work and here at the theater—and nights, too, sleeping just a few feet away from the guest rooms in his comfortable ranch-style house where he'd put her and Tyler.

Dear, sweet, solid…sexy, distracting, aggravating Trent. He made her feel all prickly inside when he caught her in the crosshairs of those steely gray eyes. And he hadn't been kidding when he'd told her a few nights earlier that a woman would know when she'd been kissed by him. After all these years—seeing him date other women, interacting with him herself—how had she missed discovering the difference between friendship and passion, between a chaste brush of his lips at her temple and that powerful stamp of perfection claiming her mouth?

And how was she was going to fit these deepening feelings for the man, this need for his strength and protection, this desire to hold and be held, back into the rules for emotional survival that had kept her safe and sane since her wild, violent and unpredictable youth? It was impossible to think of Trent as a friend while imagining what it would be like to give in to the temptation of his hard body and potent kisses again. Yet it was equally impossible to imagine how she could have gotten through this week in one piece without the friend she trusted implicitly at her side.

When she focused in on her reflection again, she realized she was stroking her own lips—missing, wishing, hungry for Trent's mouth on hers.

Good grief. Katie's cheeks flushed with emotion and she drew her fingers away from her sensitized lips. She was doing exactly what she'd told herself over and over that she shouldn't. She wasn't just attracted to Trent. She wasn't just turning to him as her cop friend to protect her from a dangerous situation. This wasn't just gratitude for helping her and Tyler time and again. She was falling for Trent Dixon. Falling for the vital, mature man her boy next door had become.

Laughter and the voices of numerous conversations and complaints woke Katie from her bothersome thoughts. Doug must have dismissed the cast and crew for the night, and they were making a mass exodus out the back workroom to the parking lot. Sliding her fingers through her loose hair, she pulled the waves off her face and groaned at the static electricity in the air that left her looking as if she'd just crawled out of bed instead of neatly downplaying the amorous turn of her thoughts. No amount of smoothing could give her a business-as-usual appearance, so she simply turned away from the mirror and hurried into the men's dressing room to pull the costumes that still needed ironing before anyone came in and questioned the embarrassed heat in her cheeks.

She exchanged smiles and a quick good-night with a few of the actors who'd left their coats or purses in the dressing rooms as she carried an armload of shirts and two of the specialty costumes out into the greenroom. She draped the shirts over the back of a chair and shook out the long black robe that belonged to the Spirit of Christmas Future.

A shadow fell over her as she spread the drapey material over the ironing board. Katie gasped, startled by the man in black standing between her and the exit door. She put her hand over her racing heart and dredged up a polite smile. "Hey, Francis."

His beady dark eyes didn't smile back. "I don't want any wrinkles in that, understand? I want it to flow as I move, so it looks as though I'm floating across the stage."

She watched the expressive gesture of his hand that demonstrated the undulating movement. "I do my best to make you all look good."

"And I appreciate that. I know I come across as a bit of a demanding actor, but my drive stems from wanting to put on the best production possible." His Adam's apple bobbed up and down as if the next few words were difficult to get out. "Your costumes have helped us achieve that."

Really? A compliment from Francis? "Thank you." He probably expected her to say something nice in return. "And, I must say, you're a very convincing Christmas spirit."

He clasped his hands behind his back, but left little more than the width of the ironing board between them. She didn't know if he was watching to make sure she pressed his costume to his specifications or if he was so socially inept that he was unaware of how his proximity and the musky smell of a long night under stage lights filling the air between them could make her feel so uncomfortable. "It was nice to have you backstage tonight, Katie. Not out in the audience where you distract Douglas."

So much for trying to get along with the man. Her hand fisted around the handle of the iron. "This again? Francis, what did I ever do to you? I'm a volunteer. I love doing theater. My son has made new friends and he's enjoying himself. I'm not looking for a relationship with any man here, and I'm certainly not interested in Doug."

"Protest all you want," he articulated in a disbelieving whine. "I see right through your little helpless-female-with-the-big-blue-eyes-and-perky-boobs act. Douglas doesn't want you for anything other than the thrill of the chase. And maybe to get lucky. If you're looking for a husband, I promise, he'll run as far from you as he can get."

"That's insulting. I am a self-sufficient woman. I have a career. I'm raising my son."

"That's probably why he cast him. Douglas took one look at you in auditions and—"

Katie shoved the iron at him, coming close enough to move him out of her space. "Shut up, Francis, or I will brand you."

"How quaint. Resorting to violence in a meager effort to defend yourself. I was only trying to give you a friendly warning."

"There's nothing friendly about these conversations. You want something from me. You're jealous or insecure or—"

"Heed my words." He leaned toward the ironing board again, perhaps sensing she wouldn't really make contact. "You're not the first pretty woman he's hit on, and you won't be the last. If you're thinking you'll be cast in a show, or your son will get a better part the next time

Douglas directs, you're mistaken. I know how power attracts women, and he's using his to entice you."

"He's not a CEO, he's directing a play." Katie plunked the iron down on the collar of his robe, ready to char an ugly hole straight through the heavy cotton if he said one more derogatory thing. She knew all about bullies like Francis. She'd grown up with one. "You need to heed *my* words. I am not the least bit tempted to sleep with Doug or whatever distasteful thing you're insinuating. If he turns you on so much, you can have him. With my blessing."

"You crazy..." Francis grabbed her wrist and the iron, snatching them away from the smell of singed material. "Stop what you're doing!"

"What?" Anger morphed into fear in a single breath. His particular choice of words surprised her far more than the pinch of his fingers on her skin. Katie tugged at his grip. "What did you say?"

"I said to stop what you're—"

"Mom!" Tyler ran across the greenroom, dropping his book bag at the argument he'd walked in on and dashing around the end of the ironing board to stand beside her and pull on her arm. Oh, Lord. Her little man thought Francis was hurting her. "Are you ready to leave? I am."

"Tyler—"

Francis set the iron down but left his fingers clamped over Katie's wrist. "Back off, Tiny Tim. I'm having a conversation with your mother."

"Not anymore you're not." A deeper voice entered the argument and ended it. Francis's eyes had barely widened with alarm before Trent was prying his grip off Katie's wrist.

Then he went up on his toes as Trent pinned Francis's

arm behind his back. "How dare you?" he sputtered through his bushy black beard.

"Don't make me take you in for assault and harassment, Sergel." Trent carried the vile man several steps away before positioning himself between her and Francis. The width and height of his shoulders and back completely blocked Francis from her line of sight. If the no-nonsense authority in his tone wasn't enough, Katie could well imagine the *just try something* challenge in Trent's expression that would keep any smart man at bay. "Whatever your beef with Katie might be, it ends now."

"I'll thank you kindly to keep your hands off me, Detective."

"I will if you keep your distance from Miss Rinaldi."

"Very well." Francis was rubbing his shoulder when he crossed the room to pick up his coat. "But don't say I didn't warn you, Katie." Francis pulled on his long black coat. "Don't trust Douglas. There's been something wrong with this entire production. Strange things happening. People who don't belong hanging around. He hasn't been himself. You and your son are the only thing different about this show and any other play I've done with him."

"Shut up, Sergel. Or Reinhardt or whatever your name is." Trent took a step toward him, and Francis hurriedly grabbed his hat and scarf. "Not one more harsh word to this boy, either. Understand?"

With a dramatic harrumph and flourish of his long dark coat, Francis swept out of the room.

Trent turned. His gaze went straight to the wrist Katie was mindlessly massaging. "Everyone okay in here?"

Katie nodded. Physically, she was fine. But her brain kept flashing with images of messages scratched in the snow or smeared in lipstick. "Francis told me to stop what I'm doing."

"What do you mean?" He reached over the ironing board and scrubbed his palm along the top of Tyler's head, reminding her son that the tension in the room had been neutralized and he could drop his guard and be a kid again.

Katie dropped her arm around Tyler's shoulders and hugged him against her hip, reassuring him with the same message, even though her mind was still racing with suspicion. "He used the exact same words—*Stop what you're doing.* That's just a coincidence, right? Do you think he could really hate or resent me so much that he would want to scare me by hiring that private detective or sending those threats?"

He nodded, giving her misgivings careful consideration. "I don't know. The threats could be some kind of weird jealousy thing—there's certainly something about that prima donna that's not right. But my money's still on Asher and your research." He crossed to the sofa to pick up his coat and shrug into it. "I'll make sure Sergel leaves. You get all your gear packed so we can get out of this place ASAP." After adjusting the hem of his short coat over his holster and badge, he plucked Francis's black robe off the ironing board and tossed it into the men's dressing room. "And forget about ironing that jackass's costume."

Tyler squinched up his face in curious frown. "Mom, what's a jackass?"

Katie squeezed her lips together to stifle her laugh at the innocent question. But a smile erupted anyway, and she walked Tyler around the ironing board to Trent. "You can explain that one, Detective."

"Sorry."

The stricken look on his rugged face stretched her smile farther. Feeling strengthened by his presence and taking pity on his uncharacteristic distress, Katie braced a hand on Trent's shoulder and stretched up on tiptoe. She didn't second-guess the impulse—she simply did what felt like the right thing to do. She slipped her fingers beneath his collar and slanted his head down to seal her lips over his. She might have started the kiss, but his warm, firm lips quickly moved over hers, completing it. The kiss was brief, and the link between the two of them warmed Katie all the way down to her toes. Trent's eyes were smiling above hers when he lifted his head. "So that's what I have to do to get your attention? Get in trouble?"

"You've always had my attention, Trent. I guess it's just taken me a long time to work up the courage to do something about it."

He combed his fingers through her hair and tucked it behind her ear. "I'm willing to take it slow, as long as I know you're on the path with me."

When he leaned in to kiss her again, they both suddenly became aware of the nine-year-old tilting his gaze from one to the other, silently observing the teasing, intimate exchange.

Trent cleared his throat and pulled away, probably worried that he was going to have to explain what was happening between his mother and best friend, too. "Mom, did you mail my letter to Santa?" Tyler asked.

Katie offered a nervous chuckle in lieu of an answer. What was going through that wise little man's mind now? "It's getting late."

Trent nodded. With a hand on her son's shoulder, he scooped up Tyler's book bag and coat and marched him toward the door. "I'll keep Tyler busy so you can finish up faster."

"Sounds like a plan."

He nodded and helped Tyler into his blue coat. "Come on, buddy. Let's bundle up."

"Is *jackass* a naughty word?" Tyler asked, following his big buddy into the backstage area without question.

"Let's talk."

Several minutes later, Katie had unplugged the iron and hung up the shirts, and even Francis's wrinkled costume, when her phone vibrated in the pocket of her jeans. She pulled it out to read a text from Trent.

We're outside. Distracting Ty with snowball fight. Hurry. I'm losing.

Grinning, Katie pulled on her stocking cap and coat and looped her flowered bag over her shoulder before texting a response.

Thanks. On my way. Duck. ;)

She knew a split second of panic when she turned off the light in the greenroom and stepped into the darkness backstage. The work lights were off on the stage and the running lights had been disconnected. She was in utter darkness. Her audible gasp echoed through the storage and work space.

"Is someone there?" a voice asked. Doug Price. As much as she hated to cast him as any kind of rescuer, she couldn't stand to be trapped in the dark again.

"Hello?" she called out. "Please tell me you're near a light switch."

She heard a shuffle of movement, and then a light came on by the exit door. Doug had set his briefcase on a chair and opened it to stuff his director's notebook inside and pull out his cap and gloves. "Over here, Katie. I'm sorry. I thought I was the last one here. I was just locking up."

What had he been doing that he hadn't seen the ambient light from the greenroom on the opposite side of the stage when she'd opened the door? And how had he made his way through the darkness back here? Ultimately, it didn't matter. She just wanted out of this place. "I'm sure I'm the last one now. Thanks for waiting."

Katie wove her way through the prop tables and set pieces that had been such obstacles in the darkness. Not that she completely trusted Doug after the things Francis had said, but she was anxious to get out into the open, eager to get to Trent and her son. But as Doug pulled his keys from the briefcase, they caught on some papers inside, and a thick manila envelope folded in half dropped out. Katie bent down to pick it up. It was heavy, as though there was a stack of large photographs or a couple of magazines inside. "Here. You dropped—"

"I'll take that." Doug snatched it from her hand. He quickly stuffed it into his briefcase and closed it. He took a deep breath, calming the brief outburst. "I'm sorry. Thank you."

Perhaps she was broadcasting her discomfort at being alone with the man, because Doug offered her a courteous nod and pushed open the steel door to a blast of swirling flakes and cold air. "Is it snowing again?" she asked.

"I think it helps set the mood for the play, don't you agree?" Hearing the squeals of a laughing child carried on the wind, Katie quickly slipped out past Doug. She spotted Trent and Tyler down by the footbridge, pelting each other with snowballs. She smiled and headed toward them, considering joining the fun, when Doug turned the key in the lock. "Hold up, dear. I'll walk you to your car."

Trent saw her and waved just before a dollop of snow hit the middle of his chest. He scooped Tyler up off his feet and jogged up the hill as Katie made her excuses. "That's very gallant of you, Doug. But my friend Trent is still here."

"Yes, of course." He switched his briefcase to the opposite hand, away from Trent's approach.

Maybe there was nothing suspicious about his behavior at all, and she was the one being paranoid. "Well, thanks. Only one rehearsal left."

Doug nodded. "We have a great show. Remember the cast party this weekend. I'd love to see you there." Trent arrived and set Tyler on his feet. The two were a pair of snow-dusted clothes and ruddy cheeks, demanding she smile at their boyish behavior. Doug seemed less amused. "You're welcome to come along, too, Detective. If you like that sort of thing."

Trent clapped his gloved hands together, throwing out a cloud of snow. "Oh, I love a good party."

"Yes, well, good night." Doug brushed away the few snowflakes that had fallen onto his shoulders and walked around the corner of the building to his car. She heard his engine start before she would have expected and the cold motor shifting into gear before driving away in a rush.

"It's a good thing he's a director," Trent deadpanned, "because he's not a very good actor. I don't believe he really wants me to come to your cast party."

"I guess he's in a hurry to find another date, then." Katie laughed out loud, feeling the stress of the day and those disturbing encounters with Francis Sergel and Doug

Price dissipate. She dropped her arm around Tyler's shoulders, linked her elbow with Trent's and led the way to the parking lot. "Come on, you two. Let's get your truck warmed up before all that snow soaks through to your skin and freezes you."

But she slowed her steps when she saw the other two cars left in the lot. They weren't campus police vehicles, and everyone else from the play had left already. Hadn't they? She eyed the silver sedan with the tinted windows parked near the exit, and the small black car parked beneath the nearest street lamp. Its engine was running, as though someone had parked close to the theater and was waiting to pick up a passenger. Only there was no driver inside.

She didn't have to be a cop to know that something wasn't right. "Trent? Doug and I were the last ones out of the theater."

Trent's hand on her arm stopped her. He pulled out his keys and thrust them into her hand. "Get in my truck and lock yourself inside."

He lifted his coat and pulled out his gun, too. Katie automatically pulled Tyler away from the weapon. "Trent?"

"Black sports car." He braced his gun between his hands and pointed it toward the car with the running engine. "The license plate matches. Call Max and tell him I located John Smith's car."

The man who'd tried to break into her apartment. "That's him? Why is he—"

"Go." Trent waved her toward his pickup and circled around to approach the car from the rear.

Katie hugged Tyler to her side and backed away. But not before she saw the hand on the steering wheel.

A bloody hand.

"Trent?" She pushed Tyler behind her and inched forward with a ghoulish curiosity. The man was injured. He needed help. No, she just needed answers. She wanted to ask him why he'd been terrorizing her. "Oh, my God."

There'd be no answers tonight. She saw the body slumped over in the front seat. She saw all the blood on his clothes and the car's upholstery.

She clutched Tyler's face against her chest and spun him away from the gruesome sight as Trent opened the car door and checked for a pulse. "Is that John Smith? Is he…?"

Trent nodded and pulled up his coat to holster his weapon. He held up two fingers, indicating the man had been shot twice, and mouthed the word *dead*.

"What's going on?" Tyler's question came from the face muffled against her breast. "Is that guy sleeping?"

With a heart that was heavy with the knowledge that her son had been anywhere close to this kind of violence, Katie exchanged a silent message with Trent and pulled Tyler toward the heavy-duty pickup with her.

"Katie! Get down!"

Katie heard three little whiffs of sound before Trent came charging around the sports car. By the time she saw the tiny explosions of snow spitting up from the pavement and heard a car door slam, Trent's arms were around her and Tyler, pushing them into a run. "Go, go, go! Run, buddy!"

Someone by the silver car was shooting at them.

When the side mirror shattered, Katie screamed. Trent swept Tyler up into his arms and grabbed Katie's hand, jerking her into a detour from the path of the bullets. "Into the trees!"

Mimicking his crouched posture, Katie pumped her

legs as fast as they would go. They zigzagged over the open pavement, taking the shortest path to cover. Katie nearly toppled when they plunged into the snow beyond the curb. It suddenly felt as if she was running in water, pulling her boots out of the sucking, frozen drifts. A bare branch splintered beside them, shooting icy crystals and shards of wood into their faces. Trent muttered a curse and jerked them away from the pelting cascade. She felt the blow of something hard against her hip and stumbled, but Trent's strong arm held her upright and kept her moving. When they reached the fallen trunk of an old oak, he leaped over the mound of rough wood, dead branches and snow and pulled Katie over the trunk with them.

She landed on her bottom, sinking waist-deep into a drift of snow. Trent shoved Tyler into her arms as another thwap of a bullet hit the far side of the tree trunk. "Stay down! Keep him covered!" he ordered.

Katie was already pulling Tyler beneath her, rolling onto her stomach on top of him and digging down into her bag for her phone. Trent peeked over the top of the tree trunk, drawing two more shots that smacked into the old wood before he ducked back down and drew his gun. Katie punched in 9-1-1 as Trent rose up again and fired off several rounds.

"Mom?" Tyler held his hands over his ears. She felt him jerk against her with every shot Trent fired.

"Stay down, sweetie." Three more shots and the dispatcher picked up. "I'm at Williams College with Detective Trent Dixon. Behind the old auditorium. Someone in a silver car is shooting at us."

Another shot pinged off a metal light by the sidewalk, turning a silver wreath into ribbons floating to the ground. Katie stayed on the line when she heard car tires squealing for traction against the wet, freezing pavement. A car door slammed and Katie's heart squeezed in her chest when Trent pushed to his feet and climbed over the top of the tree trunk. "Stay put!"

"Trent!" Katie shouted her fear as the man who meant so much to her left the shelter of the tree and chased after the car peeling out of the parking lot. She heard pounding boot steps as the ground gave way to asphalt. There were two more shots and the screaming pitch of a car sliding around a sharp turn and speeding away into the night. Katie reported to the 9-1-1 dispatcher that she and her son were okay, but that she couldn't see if Trent or anyone else had been hurt. "There's a dead body here, too. A man who's been shot. Probably by whoever was in the silver car. Send an ambulance," she begged, feeling her extremities shiver with a mix of cold and fear. "Send everybody."

"Max!" She heard Trent's long strides approaching them again and knew he was on the phone to his partner, giving him a sitrep on the shooting.

Although the dispatcher asked Katie to stay on the line, she stuffed her phone into the pocket of her coat, keeping the connection open while she dealt with the more pressing needs of hugging her frightened son and making sure Trent hadn't been hurt. "It's okay, sweetie." She wiped the chapping tears from her baby's cheeks. "Trent?"

"Right here, sunshine." He dropped over the top of the tree trunk and squatted down beside them. He stuck his gun into the back of his jeans before pulling her and Tyler out of the snow and into his arms. "The shooting's stopped. They're gone. There were two men. I think we walked into the middle of a hit."

"What? I wonder if Doug saw it, too. Maybe that's why he drove away so fast."

"Well, he didn't stop to call the police if he did. But Max heard your call on the scanner. He's already on his way. He'll get Liv and Jim moving, too, and notify the lab about our extensive crime scene. Everybody in one piece?"

Katie waited for a nod from Tyler before answering, "Wet, cold and scared out of our minds. But we're fine."

They were all on their feet now, making their way to the sidewalk and up the easier path to the parking lot. Moving forward and scanning the area for any other unwanted surprises never stopped until they reached Trent's disabled truck. Besides the shattered mirror, he had two flat tires and a cracked window. He opened the passenger door on the side away from most of the damage and reached inside to check a hole in the dashboard. "Good. We'll be able to get ballistics and have some concrete evidence for a change. I got a partial plate on the car, too, but it was moving pretty fast." He turned to pick up Tyler and set him on the seat, facing out, away from the bullet hole. "At least we'll be out of the wind here. I'm guessing campus security will reach us first. Then we can get a door unlocked and go inside."

She could already hear the sirens in the distance. Others had probably reported the sounds of gunfire, too. A chill set in as the adrenaline started to wear off and Katie started to realize the full import of what had just happened. But as Trent straightened in the open triangle of the door and truck frame, she saw the deep rip in the sleeve of his coat and the blood soaking into the layers of insulation and cotton underneath. She grabbed him by the forearm and turned his shoulder toward the street lamp above them, on alert once more. "Trent."

He pulled at the damp material to get a better look. "Oh, man, this was my favorite coat."

Katie smacked the uninjured side of his chest. "Trent Dixon, you've been shot and you're griping about your coat?"

His leather glove was cold against her cheek. But there was nothing but heat in the quick kiss he gave her before whispering, "I'm okay. We'll fix it at home."

She held on, looking up at him, and whispered back, "You're sure?"

"The shot grazed me when we were running." He winced beneath the white clouds of his breath and glanced down at Tyler. "There's a first-aid kit in the glove compartment. Let's not worry you know who."

"Then it *is* bad." Katie instantly released him and dived inside the truck to retrieve the medical supplies.

"Barely a scratch, I promise."

But she'd raised a smart kid who knew they were talking about him. Tyler swiped at the tears that were still falling, bravely taking control of his fear and confusion. "I can go to the hospital if we have to. I'll watch Mom." He sniffed and rubbed at the red tip of his nose. Katie kissed his cheek and handed him a tissue before tearing open a box of gauze pads. "I'm not scared. But real guns are loud."

Trent squeezed Tyler's knee. "They are, buddy, aren't they? Dangerous, too."

Tyler touched the cuff of Trent's bloody sleeve. "Does it hurt?"

"It stings. It's raw skin and it burns. But like I told your mama, this isn't bad. It could have been a lot worse."

"Like that man in the car?"

Katie's breath locked up in her chest and tears burned her eyes. No sense hiding the truth from him now. She hadn't been able to protect him from violence any more than her mother had been able to protect her. Trent glanced at Katie, then hunched down in front of Tyler for a man-to-man talk.

"Guns can do terrible things, Ty." Trent held out his heavy black Glock where the boy could see it without touching it before sliding it safely back into his holster. "The safety's on now, so it can't hurt you. But when it's not..."

Tyler listened in rapt attention to every word while Katie went to work, cutting away the shreds of Trent's coat sleeve, along with the flannel and thermal cotton underneath. "But guns can save lives, too. Someday I'll teach you how to shoot one safely. Until then, you don't mess with any of them, okay?"

Tyler nodded his understanding.

"But don't worry, buddy. Tonight, they aren't going to hurt you or your mom. I'm glad you're here to back me up. You can help me keep an eye out for that silver car that drove away, in case it comes back, okay? At least until Uncle Max gets here to pick us up."

"Okay."

Before Trent could straighten, Tyler threw his arms around the big man's neck and held on as he stood. Trent wound his good arm around her son and pulled him onto his lap as he perched on the edge of the seat.

Katie let him cradle her son and reassure him that the nightmare had ended, at least for tonight. Seeing her friend being so tender and protective with Tyler allowed her to breathe a little easier, too. Trent was right—the bullet had only grazed him and hadn't ripped through muscle or bone. But it wasn't an injury that was going to stop bleeding on its own anytime soon, so she pulled out a wad of gauze and applied pressure to the wound, willing it to stop, willing this good, wonderful man who clearly meant the world to her son—and to her, she was discovering—to be safe.

By the time she'd tied a longer piece of gauze around his biceps to keep the pressure bandage in place, a campus police car was pulling up. She could see lights flashing off the buildings and trees as KCPD cars and, hopefully, an ambulance arrived on campus.

"You don't think the shooters are coming back, do you?" she asked. "Are we witnesses now?"

"They won't be back tonight," Trent stated in a hushed, sure tone that inspired confidence. "My guess is that they wanted us disabled so they could make a getaway without me following them."

But she saw that he kept his hand on the butt of his weapon, just in case.

Chapter Eleven

Katie was clean and warm after her hot shower. But even in her flannel pajamas and robe and with a pair of socks she'd borrowed from Trent on her feet, she couldn't shake the chill that permeated her from the inside out.

"They doing okay?" Trent's voice was a deep-pitched whisper in the shadows of the hallway as he stepped out of the master suite and came up behind her to peek into the guest room where Tyler slept with Padre on the long twin bed.

Trent had towel dried his short hair without putting a comb through it and had the damp terry cloth hanging around his bare neck and shoulders above the fresh jeans he'd slipped on. She could feel the heat of his shower radiating off his skin, and breathed in the enticing smells of soap and man. But still, she hugged her arms around her waist and shivered. "They shot at my son."

Trent laid his hand over her shoulder. "The EMT said he was just fine—nothing a good night's sleep and a sense of security can't fix."

She turned her cheek in to the warmth and caring he offered. "You give him that."

"I think that sense of security comes from a mom who's always been there for him."

Katie grunted a small laugh of disagreement, and the tan-and-white collie mix lifted his head at the sound. She was the reason John Smith had become a part of their lives in the first place, although KCPD still wasn't certain who had hired him or why he'd been following Katie. For all she knew, Smith had been executed because he'd failed to break into her apartment and murder her, or retrieve whatever information she'd found that Leland Asher didn't want her to. Some security. More like the magnet for trouble she'd always been.

"Katie?" Perhaps sensing the guilty direction her thoughts had taken, Trent tightened his grip on her shoulder.

But she shushed him and walked into the room to pet the skinny dog that had been a blessing for Tyler to come home to. The two had eaten a snack together and played, and had separated only long enough for Tyler to take a bath and brush his teeth. She scratched the dog around his ears, then pressed a kiss to the soft fur on top of his head. "I'm counting on you to keep an eye on our boy, okay, Padre?" Then she lifted the covers and tucked Tyler's leg beneath the quilt and pulled it up to his chin. She brushed his dark hair off his forehead and kissed his sweet, velvety skin. It was a relief to see the tears had washed away and the frown mark had relaxed with sleep. "I love you, sweetie," she whispered, then winked at the alert dog. "Good boy."

As soon as Katie backed away from the bed, Padre laid his head down over Tyler's legs and she knew her son would be watched over through the night. If only she could let go of the uncertainty of these past few days and sleep so easily.

She looked up to see the big, half-dressed man filling the doorway. The gauze and tape on Trent's shoulder stood out like a beacon in the shadows cast by the lone night-light in Tyler's room, mocking his claim that she didn't screw up relationships, that the people around her didn't get hurt.

But it was too late and she was too raw to have that discussion again. So she grasped at the friendly banter and mutual support system that had always been there between them. "Okay, mister. You're next." She nudged him out into the hallway and pulled the door partly shut behind her. "The doctor said I should replace your bandage after your shower."

She stopped in her bedroom to retrieve her bag, where she'd stowed the extra supplies the doctor in the ER had given them, then followed him through the quiet house into the en suite off the master bedroom. While Trent hung up his towel, she filled a glass with water. "Antibiotics first."

"Yes, ma'am." With a weary grin on his unshaven face, he dutifully took the pill she handed him and swallowed it.

She got the distinct feeling he was humoring her when she closed the toilet lid and had him sit so she could peel the tape off the tanned skin of his upper arm and toss it and the soiled gauze beneath it into the trash. He only winced once and never complained about the pain he must be in as she made quick work of cleansing the open wound and applying a new layer of ointment before covering the injury with a clean gauze pad. But the tape twisted and fought her as she pulled it off the roll and tried to tear the pieces she needed.

"Where are those scissors?" After securing the gauze with one mangled piece of tape, Katie squatted down to open the bag and pull out the contents inside to retrieve the smaller items that had fallen to the bottom. "Just give me a sec." Wallet. Sunglasses. Squashed breakfast bar. Laptop. Mini toy truck. "There they are…"

Katie gasped. She'd been so intent on fixing up Trent and getting back to her own bed, where she prayed a dreamless sleep would claim her, that the damage done to the cover of her laptop almost didn't register. But then she trailed her finger over the small, perfectly round dent in the metal cover. A frightening realization swept through her with such force that it made her light-headed. She wobbled and sank onto her knees. She set the laptop on the tile floor and dug into her purse again. Not for scissors this time. It was… *Oh, my God.* There. Perfectly round and just big enough to slip her finger through. A bullet hole.

"Is something broken?"

Turning, she held up her bag with her finger still sticking through the hole. "I could have been killed. Tyler could have been killed. You could have…" Her voice faded with every sentence until there was barely a breath of sound. "I don't understand why this is happening.'

"Ah, Katie." Trent tossed the bag aside and pulled her onto his lap. "Sunshine, come here."

Dressing the wound was forgotten as she curled up on top of his thighs and leaned into him. His arms came around her and wrapped her up with the heat of his body.

With her ear pressed to the strong beat of his heart, Katie shivered. "I'm so cold."

His big hands moved up and down her back and arms, creating static friction as he rubbed flannel against flannel. But even that electricity couldn't seem to pierce the shroud of despair closing in around her. "You're going into a little bit of shock. Let's get you warmed up."

When he lifted her into the air, she remembered herself. "Your arm. What if it starts bleeding again?"

"Screw that."

"I need to finish dressing it."

He carried her out of the bathroom to the king-size bed where he slept. "Right now, you just need to let me take care of you." Her toes touched the floor only long enough for Trent to pull back the covers. Then he swung her up into his arms again and set her near the middle of the bed. Before she could think to protest, he'd stretched out beside her and pulled the sheet and thick comforter up over them both. He gathered her into his arms and threw one leg over both of hers, aligning them chest to hip, with her head tucked beneath his chin and their legs tangled together. "Think of it as doing me a favor." With her arms caught between them, he pulled her impossibly closer, wrapping her up in the furnace of his body. "I need a break, sunshine. This whole investigation is wearing me out. It'd be nice to not have to worry about you getting into trouble for a little while."

She almost giggled at the teasing remark, but she was too caught up in the drugging effect of his body heat seeping into hers. The tightness in her chest eased, and the shivering abated. The longer Trent held her, the longer he whispered those deeply pitched assurances in her ear, the stronger she felt. The panic lessened. Her jumbled thoughts cleared.

He stroked his fingers through her hair, pressed a kiss to the crown. "You're safe. You're fine. Tyler's fine. And I'm too big to bring down with a piddly-ass shot like this wound."

His wound. It needed to be properly tended. Katie stiffened her arms and pushed against his chest. "Trent—"

"I'm fine, too. You stay right here. This is what *I* need, remember?"

Katie wasn't sure if she'd dozed for a little while or if lying with Trent, bundled beneath the covers to chase away the wintry chill that had derailed her for a few moments, was all the healing she needed to feel more like her normal self again. To believe again that she and her son were safe. To feel as though the mistakes of her past couldn't touch her tonight. Not in Trent's bed. Not in his arms.

It was sometime later, when the wind of a winter storm outside rattled the windowpanes and startled her awake, that Katie realized she'd never returned to her own bed. And now that she was feeling rested and warm—and she couldn't hear any sounds of a boy or dog stirring—she admitted that she didn't want to leave.

"Better?" The drowsy male voice greeted her from the pillow beside her.

Katie smiled. "Much."

"This is nice, Katie Lee Rinaldi." Trent's fingers were stroking lazy circles along her back and hip, and Katie discovered her fingers taking similar liberties across the warm skin and ticklish curls of his chest. "But you know what else I need?"

Her hand stilled and she pushed herself up onto her elbow. Did he want her to finish taping his bandage? Did he need one of the painkillers the doctor had prescribed? "What is it? Anything I can do—"

"I need you to trust me."

"I do." She leaned over him, trying to assess the message in those gunmetal eyes.

"I need you to trust us—even if it's just for tonight."

Oh. Her body tingled in anticipation. "Trent, are you asking me to—"

He silenced her question with a sweetly lingering kiss. His patience with her was as maddening as it was exquisite. His lips ignited a slow burn that seemed to travel from her mouth to every point of her body where his hips and thigh and roaming hand touched her, creating a network of pathways that crisscrossed inside her, filling her with heat and an edgy sort of desire that demanded more than easygoing kisses and tender caresses.

"I know you need me to take things slow." He combed his fingers into the dark waves of her hair that brushed against his chest and tucked them behind her ear, cupping the side of her neck. "I need your brain to help me put Leland Asher away for good, but I need something else from you, too. I need to touch you to believe I didn't almost lose you tonight. I need to feel your confidence and caring to keep me strong. I need to feel your strength, holding me, accepting everything I want to give you and be for you. I'm not just asking for sex, sunshine. I need that closeness we've always shared. I—"

She shushed him with a finger over his mouth. "I think I need that, too. I want all the things I think you can give me. For tonight."

"It'll change everything between us."

Sliding her arms around his neck, Katie fell back onto the pillow, pulling him to her. "I think it already has changed."

And then there was no more conversation. There were only hungry lips and greedy hands and Trent's muscular body moving over hers.

He unwrapped her like a gift, untying her robe, unbuttoning her pajama top. He slipped his hands inside, searing her skin with every sweeping touch, every squeeze of a breast. With his thumb, he teased the sensitive tips to tiny pebbles, generating little frissons of electricity beneath every touch, feeding the current of heat and pressure stirring deep in her womb.

Carefully avoiding his injury, Katie swept her hands over the smooth skin of his back, felt the muscles of his chest quiver and jump beneath her exploring fingers. She sampled the sandpapery line of his chin and jaw, and smiled at the responsive cord of muscle at the side of his neck that made him groan deep in his throat each time she took a nip.

True to his word, he seemed to touch every inch of her body while his wicked mouth worked its magic on hers. He tugged her pajama pants down to claim her hip with the palm of his hand and pull the most feverish part of her body into the bulge thrusting behind his zipper. When he kissed his way down her neck, Katie thrust her fingers into the damp muss of his hair, releasing a spicy scent that filled her nose. She guided his mouth to the straining peak of her breast and whimpered at the bolt of heat that arced through her.

Every kiss was a temptation. Every touch a torment. "Trent," she gasped. "Now. Please."

He threw back the covers to shuck off his jeans and shorts and sheathe himself. The chill of the night had barely cooled her skin before Trent was back, tossing aside the flannel pants she'd kicked off and settling between her legs. "There's no turning back from this," he reminded her, stealing another kiss from her swollen lips.

Katie nodded and pulled at his hips, demanding he complete what he'd started. "I've made some bad choices in my life, Trent. This isn't one of them."

She lifted her knees and he slipped inside, slowly filling her with his length. His dark gray eyes locked on to hers as he began to move. She tried to hold his loving gaze, tried to memorize every second of this stolen time together, but soon the sensation was too much. She could only feel. He slipped his hand beneath her bottom and lifted her into his final thrust. Katie closed her eyes and surrendered to the heat bursting inside her. Seconds later, Trent gasped her name against her hair and followed her over the edge into the fiery inferno.

TRENT AWOKE TO the sound of a phone ringing and an empty bed.

He swung his feet to the floor, trying to orient himself to the long night and the early hour. He scratched his fingers through his hair, instantly remembering how Katie had played with it—and how her fingers had tightened against his scalp, holding his mouth to a sweet, round breast as she gasped for breath and squirmed with delight beneath him. Hell. Even remembering how she'd put her hands all over him with such hungry abandon was enough to make things stir down south this morning.

With a groan of resignation, he scooped up his shorts and jeans, fishing his ringing cell out of the back pocket and checking the number. Olivia Watson. She'd hold for a couple more rings, giving him time to go into the john to splash some cold water on his face and try to get his head on straight before taking a work call.

He'd known Katie had a rockin' body. What fool male wouldn't want to put his hands all over those decadent curves? But he hadn't expected how responsive she'd be to every needy touch. How eager she'd be to explore him, as well. That was the free spirit he'd imagined her to be in his youth. That was the Katie who'd first captured his young heart.

And he sure as hell hadn't expected this gut kick of pain when he realized their time together—a crazy mix of comfort, caring and passion—didn't mean as much to her as it did to him. Hell. She must have left before dawn. The painkiller in his system had knocked him out eventually, and he'd slept longer than usual, oblivious to her efforts to escape and erase any evidence of their time spent together.

The phone was still ringing in his hand when he strolled back into the bedroom and sat on the black-and-gold comforter that had been draped neatly back on the bed—after he distinctly remembered it sliding off onto the floor last night. Katie hadn't left so much as a dent in the pillow beside him this morning. She'd taken every stitch of clothing, even her damaged bag and the contents that had been scattered across his bathroom floor, leaving no trace of *them* behind.

Well, he'd gotten exactly what he'd asked for, hadn't he? One night with Katie Lee in his bed. If only the two of them had been lousy together. If only the hushed conversation and cuddling in between hadn't made him think that it had meant something life changing to her, too. Trent hadn't felt that right inside his own skin for ten years. But expecting Katie to suddenly love him the way he loved her…?

The bedroom door burst open and a nine-year-old and the excited dog chasing him jumped onto the bed. "Aren't you going to answer your phone?" Tyler asked, bouncing up and down on his knees. "It's been ringing forever."

"Tyler." Katie followed a few steps after, hanging back

in the doorway. She'd already dressed in a pair of jeans and a sweatshirt and had pulled the sexy waves of her hair back into a tomboyish ponytail. "I told you not to wake Trent."

"But, Mom, he was already awake." Tyler threw himself on the bed, which bounced like a trampoline with his light weight. "Padre and I peeked."

Katie shook her head at the bouncy boy and whining dog and frowned an apology at Trent. "I didn't know if I needed to answer the phone for you."

Was this entourage the reason she'd left him this morning? Letting Tyler see the two of them share a kiss was one thing, but explaining what it meant when Mommy and Trent slept in bed together was something else. Or was that just the excuse she was using for pretending as though last night had never happened?

"Nope. I got it." He punched the button on the phone and put it to his ear. "Olivia. What's up?"

"Sorry to wake you, Sleeping Beauty, but I'm at the ME's office at the crime lab. My brother Niall just completed the autopsy on your private detective. We got an ID on John Smith."

"Hold on a sec, Liv. Katie's here with me. I'm going to put you on speakerphone." Katie hustled Tyler out of the room with orders to finish his bowl of cereal and get dressed for school. Then she nodded and came back to stand beside Trent and listen in on the call. "Tell us about John Smith. Which one of those aliases was real?"

"None of them. None of those identities existed until about ten years ago. John Smith is the most recent incarnation. The man had a knack for reinventing himself."

Normally, all the details were important. But he was

only in the mood for straight answers this morning. "You said you had a match."

"We do. His fingerprints are in the system."

Katie pulled the phone down to her level and asked, "Then why didn't this guy's real identity pop when I ran the search on him?"

"Because Niall found the prints in the archives." Katie tilted her confused frown up to meet his. The KCPD archives were the files where cases that had been solved were stored. Or where crimes that had passed their statute of limitations—meaning the police could no longer pursue them—had been filed away. "Does the name Francisco Dona ring a bell?"

Katie's encyclopedic memory came up with the connection first. "Isabel Asher's boyfriend? The guy Leland blamed for her death?" She shook her head. "There was a motorcycle accident. Francisco Dona is dead."

"He is now." Olivia's sarcasm wasn't entirely for humor's sake. "The fingerprints don't lie. This guy has been able to fly under the radar for ten years. Somehow, he got his prints in a DB file and a John Doe was cremated in his place. He was reborn as a new man several times over, most recently as John Smith, private eye."

Trent tried to have some respect for a man who could change his identity as readily and completely as the WIT-SEC division of the US Marshals' office could. But all he could see was a criminal who'd gotten far too close to Katie and Tyler. "So if he knew we were tracking Leland Asher and putting together a case against him, Francisco Dona—Mr. Smith—would have a personal stake in finding out what we know."

Olivia agreed. "If Asher found out the man he blamed for his sister's death was still alive, he'd make fixing that mistake his number-one priority once he got out of prison. He'd certainly want to make sure the man paid before the cancer got him."

That dimpled frown had reappeared between Katie's eyebrows. "I get why Francisco Dona would come after me. I'm the information guru—I'd be his best source for finding out where we are in the Asher investigation and what the team's chances are of putting him back in prison for life."

"But?" Trent prompted, wondering what wheels were turning in that clever mind of hers.

"But if he had access to my laptop, which he did when he or someone else planted the mirroring program, then why threaten me? Why warn me to stop? He should want every piece of information he could steal from me."

"Are we dealing with two different cases here?" Trent suggested. "Smith might have been after Katie, but some-body else was after Smith."

Olivia had her own idea. "Or maybe trailing Katie was Smith's effort to try to escape from Asher's retribution one more time, but he failed. Still, how did Smith get access to Katie's computer in the first place?"

Katie spoke up this time. "I have a theory on that." She glanced up at Trent, perhaps offering an explanation for her hasty retreat this morning. "A couple of weird things happened at the theater last night."

"Besides finding a dead body and getting shot at?" What else had he missed besides Francis Sergel putting his hands on Katie?

"I did some research this morning. The bullet just dented my laptop—it still works." When she gestured for him to follow, Trent went into the spare bedroom with her. He tried to ignore that all her things had been moved in here and focus on the restraining-order record she pulled up on the screen. "There have been sexual harassment complaints filed against Doug Price. I found a record of a college student who went to a judge after she discovered Doug hiding a camera in a women's dressing room and taking pictures without her consent."

Trent borrowed one of Max's choice curses. "How does this guy get to work in community theater?"

"Because it's a volunteer position with a volunteer board, and sometimes it's hard to find people with the skills to organize and run a show who are willing to give up that much of their time." Katie shrugged. "And probably because people don't talk about it enough. I've found three different theater companies where Doug has volunteered in Missouri and Kansas."

"And you think he planted the device to sabotage your computer?" Olivia asked.

"He could have been blackmailed into doing it. It fits our *Strangers on a Train* theory about someone manipulating others to commit crimes for them." Trent was less than thrilled to hear about Katie's encounter with Doug Price last night. "He was eager that I not touch or see whatever was in that envelope. I wonder if they were photographs, or copies of them. And the price to keep them from going to the police or going public was tampering with my computer."

Olivia seemed to agree it was a strong possibility. "Do you think he killed John Smith? Or Francisco? Or whatever we're calling him now?"

"I don't think he'd have the guts to pull a trigger. But maybe he saw something and that's why he was in such a hurry to leave—especially if Smith was his blackmailer."

"You want me to bring Doug Price in for questioning?" Olivia offered.

"Yeah. Put Max to work, too." Trent had a feeling that after months of hard work and dangerous setbacks, a lot of cold cases were about to break wide open. "I want to know if John Smith was tracking Katie for his own survival or if someone else hired him. If so, who? And why?"

Katie nodded. "And if last night was a hit ordered by Asher, how did he find out John Smith's real identity?"

Trent headed back to his own room. "I want Leland Asher in my interrogation room. Today."

"I'll clear it with the lieutenant and have Max pick him up."

"Katie and I will stop by Smith's office to see what we can find there before coming in."

Trent hung up and went to work, unlocking his gun from the strongbox in his closet and sliding the weapon onto his belt. He started to pull on a thermal undershirt but realized the dressing on his wound needed changing. Unfortunately, it was a two-handed project. He pulled off the twisted tape and soiled gauze and dangled it at Katie's door. "A little help?"

"Come on in." She set down the blouse and sweater she'd been getting ready to change into and picked up her bag with the first-aid supplies. He sat on the edge of the double-size bed while she doctored him. "Jim's coming by to take Tyler to school again and watch him until we pick him up. And then I'll start pulling everything KCPD has on Francisco Dona and John Smith. I'll get a brief together on Asher and his minions before you run your interviews this afternoon, so you know who all the players are."

After the first piece of tape was secured on his shoulder, Trent caught Katie by the wrist. Even if she was going to pretend it hadn't happened, he needed to say something about last night. "Damn, you smell good in the morning." He watched the blush of heat creep into her cheeks as he lightly massaged the warm beat of her pulse. "You were amazing last night. But I missed you when I woke up. I gather you don't want Tyler to know what happened."

Katie twisted her wrist from his touch and cut another length of tape. "If he doesn't know how close we got, maybe he won't get his hopes up and think—"

"That you and I could be a real couple."

She positioned the tape over the gauze and gently smoothed it into place. "Trent. Last night was like a fairy tale. Tyler had a dad and a dog, and you were completely wonderful to me."

"But?" He was wary of where this explanation was going.

"Obviously, this isn't over yet. Between a mob boss and a dead private detective, there are still so many things that could go wrong. You've already been hurt. Tyler was frightened out of his mind. And, let's face it, I wigged out on you." She picked up his thermal shirt and helped him slide his arm into the sleeve without disturbing the bandage. "I've never been part of the story where they all live happily ever after. I'm afraid a few moments like last night, that idyllic perfection, aren't real."

He pulled his shirt on over his head and slipped the rest of it into place before standing beside her. He dropped his head to whisper against her ear, "It is for me, sunshine. As far as I'm concerned, the fairy tale is real." He inched in a little farther and pressed a kiss to her hair. "I just need you to decide when or if you're going to accept that I'm in love with you and that you're in love with me. I want to be a father to your son and a husband to you. And you know damn well that I'd be good at both."

He couldn't lay it on the line any plainer than that. With his heart and future in her hands now, Trent left her standing there in pale silence and returned to his own room to put on his badge and go to work.

Chapter Twelve

What John Smith's office lacked in decor, it more than made up for in messiness.

Katie helped Trent sort through the rows of file cabinets, looking for anything useful. Folders had been stuffed into drawers without regard to labels or alphabetizing. Whoever had gone through the office before them hadn't been there to rob Smith because they'd left behind a bottle of scotch and bag of marijuana that had been stashed in the back of one drawer.

She'd at least been able to make more sense out of his desktop computer. It appeared he'd used it mainly for word processing and internet research, so she'd easily tracked several of the searches he'd recently made—including a floor plan for the units in her apartment complex, news updates on Leland Asher's release from prison and several searches of medical sites to find the prognosis and life expectancy for a sixty-year-old man diagnosed with lung cancer.

"Looks like he's been tracking Asher for years," Katie reported.

Trent nodded, looking over her shoulder to read the monitor. "That clued him in on when he needed to change his identity again. If Asher got too close to finding out he was still alive, Francisco would go underground for a few months and reinvent himself as someone else."

"The medical searches probably meant he was hoping Leland would die soon. Maybe that was why he was at the press conference, to see with his own eyes whether the man who wanted him dead had long to live."

Trent went back to the file cabinets to continue his search. "Unfortunately for him, he miscalculated. Leland's men got to him first."

Katie rolled the chair away from the desk to help Trent dig through the remaining mess for other useful clues. There was one more piece of information she could get off Smith's computer—who had hired him to spy on her— but they needed a different warrant to breach the confidential agreement between investigator and client. While Lieutenant Rafferty-Taylor pleaded their case to a warrant judge, she and Trent were spending their morning in dusty cabinets, sharing terse, business-only conversation.

"Katie." His sharp voice pulled her from her thoughts. He set a bent folder on top of the cabinet and opened it. "Is this who I think it is?"

Katie joined him, reading the name scrawled across the top of the first page. "Stephen March." She flipped through the pages to see copies of March's time spent in drug courts and rehab, along with a criminal complaint Stephen March had filed against his sister's fiancé, Richard Bratcher, which had been thrown out of court. "This shows March's motive for wanting Bratcher dead, as well as blackmailable offenses that could be used to get him to kill Dani Reese." She dug farther into the drawer in front of her. "These are all people Smith investigated?"

"Looks like it." He peeled a tiny slip of masking tape off the inside of the drawer. "I wonder."

"What is it?"

He showed her the hyphenated list of numbers before crossing over to the safe behind Smith's desk. He knelt down and twisted the numbers on the dial. "This guy was resourceful, but I don't know that he knew much about security precautions." Trent opened the door and pulled out three thick manila envelopes and stacked them on top of the safe. He pulled a fourth one out and dumped the contents out beside the stack. Out tumbled bundles of money. Twenties, fifties, hundreds. "I'm guessing this was a cash business. Probably a smart idea for a man who had to change identities and bank accounts every couple of years."

"Trent." She pulled another folder from the file drawers. "This says Hillary Wells." There were other files in this cabinet that matched names in her own research. "That creep piggybacked off all my work. In some of these, he's gone to websites I checked and printed off the exact same information." She didn't know whether to feel angry that he'd stolen her months of dedicated research to use for some nefarious purpose or violated to think John Smith, aka Francisco Dona, had followed every thought, every move, she'd made on her computer—and she hadn't even known he'd been lurking, watching.

"I think we're onto something here, sunshine."

Katie snapped out of the emotional debate. Trent hadn't used her nickname since that conversation about fairy tales earlier that morning. In fact, he'd barely looked at her. And he certainly hadn't kissed her or held her or touched her in any way since dropping that bomb of an admission this morning.

I just need you to decide when or if you're going to ac-

*cept that I'm in love with you and that you're in love with
me. I want to be a father to your son and a husband to you.*

That promise was everything she'd wanted growing
up. But a life's worth of mistakes and tragedies made it
difficult to believe in that promise. How was she supposed to do the right thing when she wasn't sure what
that was anymore? How could Trent love her enough to
risk a relationship with a woman with all her phobias and
eccentricities and emotional baggage that came with the
package? And was it worth the risk of her and Tyler losing him from their lives if the relationship didn't work?
Then again, maybe she'd lost him already by not giving
him the answer he'd wanted this morning.

And the idea of not having Trent's strong arms and
stalwart presence and beautiful soul in her life anymore
already felt like a very big mistake.

But Trent was talking work now, not their personal
lives, where she got him shot and broke his heart. She
circled around the desk to join him. "What did you find?"

He pulled another manila envelope from the safe and
handed it to her. "Check inside. I'm guessing that envelope you saw with Doug Price held something similar."

Katie pulled out a stack of photographs. "Oh, my."
These were images of scantily clad women, obviously
taken by a hidden camera. She even recognized an image
of the college student who'd sued Doug for harassment.
"Oh. My."

"You blackmail a man into doing a job for you, then
you keep an extra copy of the evidence for insurance
purposes."

Katie stuffed the pictures back inside the envelope.
"This man was horrible."

"Which one?" The phone in Trent's pocket rang before

she could answer. Katie waited in anticipation until he nodded. "Yes, ma'am." She sat at the desk again and booted up the private detective's computer, waiting for the order. "We've got the warrant. Do it."

One keystroke and she'd know who'd hired Smith to spy on her. She leaned back in the chair, surprised by the answer on the screen. "There's only one name here. One person who hired Smith to watch over all these people."

"Please tell me it's Leland Asher."

"No. Dr. Beverly Eisenbach."

TRENT GLANCED AROUND Ginny Rafferty-Taylor's office, as anxious to get this show underway as the drumming of Katie's fingers or Max's pacing would indicate.

Four suspects. Four different strategies. Four different plans of attack.

And if the team was as good as the lieutenant seemed to think, then Leland Asher would be on his way back to prison by the end of the night.

The petite lieutenant picked up the stack of folders Katie had prepared and handed them to Trent. "Are you ready to do this?"

"Yes, ma'am."

"How do you want to handle it?"

Trent glanced over to Katie's big blue eyes staring up at him. He couldn't, wouldn't put his heart out there again for her to torment until she decided whether she was going to live her life taking risks or holed up in the security of lonely nobility. But whether he got his fairy-tale ending or not, he'd be damned if anyone was going to hurt her or Tyler again.

He nodded to her, making that silent vow, and headed

out to Interview Room 1. "I'm going to pick off the little fish first."

In the grand scheme of things, Doug Price was an easy interrogation. Trent was twice the older man's size, and all he had to do was stand and dominate the room to get the play director to talk.

He tossed the stack of lewd photos he'd gotten from John Smith's safe and fanned them across the table in front of Doug and his attorney. "Anything look familiar to you, Mr. Price?"

His lawyer tried to keep Doug from saying anything, but the man already had some of that oversprayed hair falling out of place. He sat forward in his chair. "Where did you get these?"

Trent tossed a crime-scene photo of John Smith's bloody face on top of the other pictures. "From this guy."

Doug cringed and pushed the photos away. But he cracked like an egg. "John Smith. He's a private investigator. He told me he'd given me the last copies of those pictures when I saw him last night. I had no reason to kill him. I was doing him a favor." A favor in the sense that Smith hadn't given Doug any choice. "Smith said if I kept an eye on Katie and helped him get access to your team's investigations that he wouldn't turn any of those photos over to the police."

"So you sabotaged Katie's laptop and left those threats for her? You assaulted her in the women's dressing room?"

"It wasn't assault. I was removing a camera. I wasn't expecting her to be there. I just wanted to get away."

"I think we can safely say that your career in community theater is over." Trent pulled out a chair on the opposite side of the gray metal table. Doug started to relax, but Trent decided to stay on his feet and catch him off guard. He pulled three more photographs from the file Katie had prepared. Three more links in the chain of related crimes she'd dug up in her extensive research. He set the pictures down in front of Doug, one by one. "Do you know any of these people?"

"No. No." He pointed to the last one. "Her. I don't understand what she has to do with any of this."

Interesting. "Who is she to you, Doug?"

"My therapist. I saw Dr. Eisenbach for a few months years back. Court-ordered sessions. The judge said I had an addiction to pornography."

BEV EISENBACH AND Matt Asher clammed up behind their attorneys when they were separated into two interview rooms. But as Olivia slyly observed when she and Max *accidentally* allowed the two suspects' paths to cross in the hallway across from the restrooms, the twenty-two-year-old and the woman old enough to be his mother clearly knew each other. They'd called each other by their first names in a quick, hushed conversation, and their fingers had met in a quick squeeze.

Now, there was an odd couple.

They each truthfully claimed to have shared nothing with Trent, then whispered something about promising to remain silent.

So the two had a plan that they'd clearly been working on together for some time…while their uncle/boyfriend had been locked away in prison. Instead of kowtowing to the boss, they'd been plotting behind his back. Setting Leland up for murder? Or taking over the criminal empire from a dying man?

The information Olivia had fed Trent between interviews made him grin. Bev and Matt's conversation had given Trent some key intel to use as he moved on to his final interview with Leland. He grinned because while they acted as though Leland was on his way out of the business, and they were setting themselves up to take his place, someone had forgotten to tell Leland.

Trent's approach to a man of Leland Asher's self-appointed stature was different than the intimidation he'd used with Doug Price or the friendly charm he'd turned on his nephew and Bev Eisenbach. "How long do you have to live, Mr. Asher? Years? Months? Weeks?"

Leland smiled. "I like a man who's direct, Detective. I can talk to a man like that."

Trent leaned forward in his chair, matching Leland's confident posture. "Did you have any dealings with Craig Fairfax at the penitentiary infirmary?"

"Fairfax?" Leland scratched at his gaunt cheeks. "Poor bloke. Terrible cough. I always thought he was going to hack up a lung. Very difficult to have a conversation with him."

"So you did interact with him. Did you ever talk about Katie Lee Rinaldi?"

"Who?"

Trent steeled his gazed on Asher, knowing Katie was watching in Lieutenant Rafferty-Taylor's office through the closed-circuit camera overhead. This would be a tough line of questioning for her to hear, but since she was part of the team, she'd insisted on listening in. "A girl Fairfax kidnapped ten years ago."

"Oh, that Katie. Tragic upbringing from what I hear. Yes, I believe she's the district attorney's daughter now." Close enough. Apparently, Fairfax had been filling Asher in on Katie's family history. "Goodness knows, Mr. Fairfax has a vendetta against that man. If he could get out of prison, I'm sure his first stop would be the DA's house, or perhaps his wife's school—or at the home of this Katie you mentioned. Yes, I remember he definitely has a score he wants to settle...*if* he were ever to be released from prison."

Trent's hand fisted beneath the table at the indirect but abhorrent threats, although he betrayed nothing to Asher. "Do you have a score to settle, Mr. Asher? With Francisco Dona, perhaps?"

"I have no comment."

"What about John Smith? Do you know anyone by that name?"

"Not very original, is it?" Trent waited until Leland answered the question. "No, I don't believe I do."

"But you know Dona."

"Knew, Detective. Past tense. Dona died in a motor-cycle accident several years ago."

"Did he?" Trent wasn't intimidated by the man's condescending tone. "If you discovered Mr. Dona was alive after all these years, you'd want to do something about it, wouldn't you?"

Leland checked his brittle nails before leaning forward and resting the elbows of his tailored suit on the table. "I liked you better when you were straightforward, Detective. You know as well as I do that Francisco is a sensitive subject for me. He turned my sister on to drugs and then killed her with them. At the very least, he was a coward and let her die without raising a finger to help. Isabel was the light of my life. Francisco snuffed that light out."

He wanted straightforward? "Did you murder Francisco Dona last night in retaliation for your sister's death? Or hire someone to murder him?"

"So he is dead." Asher leaned back in his chair and

smiled. "I'm a dying man. Whether it was ten years ago or yesterday, knowing he died before me makes me very happy."

Leland checked his watch and glanced at his attorney. "Will there be anything else, Detective Dixon? I have a dinner engagement I don't want to miss."

"Just one last question and then I can let you go."

"What's that?"

"Did you know that your girlfriend, Beverly Eisenbach, and your nephew, Matt, have been having an affair while you've been incarcerated in Jefferson City?"

Leland leaned over to whisper something with his attorney before answering.

"Yes."

KATIE KNEW SOMETHING was terribly wrong when the cast came out for curtain call at the final dress rehearsal. There were only five Cratchit children crossing to center stage. Where was Tiny Tim? "Where's Tyler?"

She ran down to the stage and straight up the stairs, pushing aside actors while the music was playing and they were still taking their bows. She wasn't going to lose him again.

"Wyatt? Kayla? Have you seen Tyler?"

The other children seemed startled to realize one of them was missing.

"No, ma'am."

"We were playing cards backstage at intermission. He said his last line, didn't he?"

Yes, her son had the last line of the entire show. Then the actors had all exited backstage to line up for bows, and now... "Francis." She caught the tall actor by the sleeve of his robe before he went back onstage. "Have you seen my son?"

She heard him snorting beneath his mask. "No director. Missing actors. Crazy costume ladies dashing across the stage. You know what they say—a bad dress rehearsal means we'll have a stellar opening night."

"Stuff it, Francis. Have you seen Tyler?" He tugged his robe from her grasp and ignored her question. "Then is Trent here yet?"

Francis snickered from behind his mask. "It's not my job to keep track of your child or that bruiser boyfriend of yours."

"Francis, please."

"That's my cue."

Trent had promised to be here by the end of the rehearsal. Maybe Trent had arrived early and he and Tyler had gotten to talking backstage and her son had simply missed his cue. Katie hurried back to the greenroom.

He'd had to stay late at the precinct office, walking Doug Price through booking, writing up reports on his interviews with Leland and Matt Asher and Beverly Eisenbach, and sitting down with the rest of the team to determine whether they had enough circumstantial evidence for arrest warrants yet. Normally, Katie would have been part of such a meeting, but Lieutenant Rafferty-Taylor had excused her for Tyler's benefit. With the threat of John Smith no longer in the picture, Katie had figured she could go to the final dress rehearsal without the benefit of a 24/7 bodyguard. Even so, Trent had insisted a uniformed officer accompany them, and he'd promised to join them at the theater as soon as he could get away from work. After all, Tyler still wanted him to be a part of his life, even if Katie needed time to decide how to respond to Trent's ultimatum.

But maybe that need for an evening of independence to figure out her future had been a mistake.

She hurried past Ebenezer Scrooge himself, knowing there would be no other actors behind him. The crew members thought Tyler was onstage or had made an emergency run to the bathroom and forgotten he had to go back out.

She found Tyler's street clothes still on the hanger in the men's dressing room, although his coat was gone.

Katie quickly slipped into her own coat and pulled out her phone. He wouldn't have been so foolish as to go out and play in the snow, would he? Just in case, she hurried across the backstage area and stepped outside. "Tyler?"

Not trusting her son's safety to anyone else, Katie punched in Trent's number and lifted the phone to her ear. It rang once before she saw the silver car, just like the night before, waiting in the crowded parking lot. She saw Leland Asher nod to her before climbing into the backseat. "Oh, no. Tyler!"

She started to run. But strong arms locked around her from behind, knocking her phone into the snow and lifting her off the ground. A rough hand and a pungent cloth muffled her scream, and within seconds, her knees grew weak and the world faded into black.

THE NIGHTMARE DIDN'T go away when Katie awoke.

It had just taken on warmer temps and a posher backdrop.

She was still a prisoner, like she'd been at seventeen. And her beloved little boy was once again in harm's way.

Instead of being handcuffed to a bed in a makeshift

hospital ward, waiting to deliver a baby, she was seated at Leland Asher's ornate walnut desk in the study of his mansion, hacking into a computer system for him. She didn't need to be drugged or kept in chains in order to cooperate. The two thugs who'd kidnapped her and Tyler had already shown her Matt Asher's dead body and promised to do the same to her nine-year-old son if she didn't do their boss's bidding.

There was something seriously twisted inside Leland Asher's head to make him order his bodyguards to lure Tyler outside the theater with a story about her getting hurt in the parking lot. Now he had them tie Beverly Eisenbach to a brocaded Queen Anne chair before thanking them for their years of service and dismissing them, promising each a healthy bonus in their bank accounts. Then he'd kissed his longtime girlfriend and stuffed his wadded-up handkerchief into her mouth to muffle her protests and pleas for mercy. With Matt Asher dead, Leland weakened by his illness and the hired help dismissed for the night, Katie even briefly considered standing up to Leland herself, maybe shoving the desk chair at him and making a run for it with Tyler, or whacking him over the head with this computer.

But as if sensing her tendency to tempt fate, he used the one thing she cared about most to force her to unlock code and break through firewalls and search through servers to access the information he wanted—he stood in the center of the room framed by windows and floor-to-ceiling curtains and simply rested one hand over the shoulder of her son and held a gun in the other.

Her sinuses reeled with a headache from the knockout chemical they'd used on her, but her synapses were firing on all cylinders. She'd been at the computer for about an hour since getting her instructions, but in reality, she'd gained access to Beverly's medical files within the first fifteen minutes. She'd spent the rest of the time fighting for survival in the best way she knew how. She prayed her desperate plan had worked and that it had worked quickly enough for her and Tyler to have a chance to escape.

She rested her fingers for a moment before looking up at the gray-haired man. "I'm in."

"I want you to access her private files."

Beverly screamed through her gag, rocking back and forth in her chair, pulling at the ropes that bound her.

"I need a warrant to do that," Katie explained.

Leland put the gun to Tyler's head and Katie bit her lip to stop from crying out. "Here's your warrant. Now do it."

Katie's fingers sailed over the keyboard again. "You keep looking at me, Tyler. Think about Padre. He's going to need you to give him some extra exercise tonight because we'll be getting home so late." She locked her gaze on to Tyler's red-rimmed eyes and smiled. "You focus right here, sweetie. I love you. Don't ever forget that, not for one second." He wiped his nose on the sleeve of his costume and nodded, trying so hard to be brave and remain calm for her.

She glanced down at her work, wanting to do everything she could to maintain Tyler's focus on her and keep him from witnessing a gruesome crime or becoming a victim himself.

Don't make a mistake. Don't make a mistake.

Since Leland hadn't questioned anything she'd done so far, Katie pretended the extra commands she typed in were necessary to retrieve the sensitive information that the law and a stubborn girlfriend wouldn't give him. The counseling office's patient list was already on her screen. But with her fingers flying over the keyboard, she embedded a message and sent it to Trent's phone. The message was sent and gone by the time she'd reached Bev Eisenbach's confidential files.

"Have you finished yet?" Leland was growing impatient.

She couldn't push her luck too much further. "Just about."

Leland kept his grip on Tyler but switched the gun back to Beverly as tears smeared her mascara and she whimpered for forgiveness. "Miss Rinaldi, I remind you that I'm a dying man."

"I'm in the system." *Find us, Trent. Find us.* "I'm pulling up the patient files now. What do you want me to look for?"

Leland smiled, pleased with her success. Keeping a grip on Tyler's arm, he walked over to Beverly and pulled the gag from her mouth. "It was quite a clever plan all those years ago that you came up with, darling. Care to explain yourself?"

Bev coughed for a few seconds before she could speak. "Leland, dearest, you know I've always had your best interests at heart. Look at all I've done for you. I convinced that tweaking drug addict to kill that reporter who was going to expose your connections to the senator. I did the world a service by having your men kill Lloyd Endicott so that Dr. Wells would murder that horrible Richard Bratcher. I found out Francisco Dona was still alive. I found out he was working as a private detective."

"No. No, dear. You kept that from me." He drew the gun across Beverly's forehead, and Katie nearly screamed at the horrible images he was exposing her son to. "All these years I thought I'd avenged Isabel's death, only to find out that my nephew—her own son—knew he still breathed air, and you two hadn't done a damn thing about it. I had to have my men take care of it."

Katie was a bit of a brilliant geek herself. She'd already tapped into her KCPD account and was mirroring everything that she was doing here on the department server. She'd pinged Trent's phone—Max's, Olivia's and Jim's, as well. Lieutenant Rafferty-Taylor received a notification of the new files uploading. Katie had even copied a notice to her surrogate father, the DA.

Look at Miss Katie Lee Rinaldi—taking a huge risk, bending the rules, doing whatever was necessary to protect the people she loved. She was charging into battle, taking on a known criminal to save her son and her own life one more time.

Read between the lines, Trent. Find us.

She'd always been able to get herself into trouble, but Trent would always be there to help her get out of it—to catch her when she fell, when she was frightened, when she was terrified her next mistake might cost her everything she held dear.

Be patient with me a little longer, babe. I love you. I need you. I'm in love with you.

A loud crash at the front door shook through the house. "KCPD! We're coming in!"

Tyler cried out with a startled yelp.

"It's okay, Ty," she reassured him. "They're using a battering ram to break down the door."

"At last." Leland smiled from ear to ear. "I wondered how long it would take the police to find you."

"Asher!" A deep, familiar voice echoed through the house.

"Mom!" Tyler recognized Trent's voice, too. She saw him pull from Leland Asher's grasp.

She put up her hand, cautioning him to obey. "Shh, sweetie. Remember you're playing a part. You're the good little boy who does whatever Mr. Asher says, right?"

Tyler's frightened eyes locked on to hers again and he nodded.

The next voice Katie heard was Ginny Rafferty-Taylor's. "Leland Asher. Your house is surrounded. Your chauffeur and bodyguards have been neutralized. It's just you and me and a lot of very angry cops."

"I'd be happy to talk with you, Lieutenant."

The team must be working its way through the mansion while the lieutenant stalled Asher. "I need to talk to the hostages first. I need to know they're okay."

"Are you?" Leland tightened his grip on Tyler's collar and Katie nodded. "Answer her."

"It's Katie, Lieutenant. Tyler and I are both fine. But Mr. Asher has a gun."

Leland laughed. "Of course I have a gun. All your police friends have guns—it's only fair. Please. Welcome to my home, Lieutenant."

Oh, God. Now his bizarre actions made sense. "He wants you to come in. He wants… Oh, God, please don't hurt my son."

"Did you find the evidence I requested, Miss Rinaldi?" Tears stung her eyes and she reached out for Tyler. "Miss Rinaldi."

She forced her attention back to the computer. "Yes. Dr. Eisenbach has notations in her patient files. Those with secrets she can use to blackmail them, those who need a favor and will do something in exchange for that favor." What more did the man want from her? "Could I please have my son?"

The lieutenant's voice sounded closer when she spoke

again. "Are you sure everyone is okay? Your nephew is here. He's been shot, Mr. Asher. He's dead."

"Yes, I did that."

He was confessing to murder with dozens of cops swarming the estate? With three witnesses who could testify against him right here?

Katie was more certain than ever that this monster intended to commit suicide by cop. He was a dying man, determined to set his affairs in order—to eliminate those who'd betrayed him and then die instantly himself, avoiding a lingering death.

But with her innocent boy smack-dab in the middle of all those guns? She couldn't let that happen.

"Don't shoot! Please don't shoot! There's an innocent child here." Katie reached out again. "Please, Mr. Asher. May I have my son?"

"Soon, Miss Rinaldi." He turned his attention to Tyler. "Would you like to go over and sit with your mother?"

"Yes, please."

"When she's done working. She's proven more loyal to her loved ones than my family has been to me." Leland looked around the room, perhaps seeing the movement of SWAT cops taking position outside the windows. "Did you find the information I was looking for, Miss Rinaldi? Has my beloved Beverly betrayed me?"

Katie looked at the incriminating evidence she'd pulled off Dr. Eisenbach's computer records. The notations Leland Asher had asked her to find were right there.

Francisco Dona, aka John Smith, is alive. Can use him to eliminate threats and provide surveillance to ensure jobs are completed as ordered in exchange for keeping his identity from Leland.

Matt Asher's hatred for his uncle can be used to my advantage. String him along with promise of helping him take over the business. He can do the dirty work and I can reap the profit. (I've earned it.)

Stephen March, Hillary Wells, Doug Price and many more—their names were all there. The psychologist had counseled all of them, forced them to do her bidding, first to please Leland—to become an indispensable ally with hopes of eventually becoming his wife or business partner—and later to eliminate Leland himself when his promises of power and position turned out to be lies.

But once Katie gave Leland the information he wanted, the bullets would start to fly. And Tyler—her son, her angel—would be caught in the crossfire.

"Miss Rinaldi. My time is running short. I'm sure your compatriots are closing in on my position and lining up kill shots even as we speak. Is the information there? Did my love betray me?"

Beverly wept in her bonds, begging to make amends. "Leland, please."

"Miss Rinaldi?"

Katie pointed to her face, silently telling Tyler not to look anywhere else, to hold fast to the love in his mother's eyes.

"Miss Rinaldi?"

"Yes. It's all here. Beverly and Matt have betrayed you."

"Thank you."

Without missing a beat, Leland shoved Tyler toward Katie. Beverly screamed as he turned and fired a bullet right into the middle of her forehead.

Katie lunged for her son and wrapped him in her arms,

dragging him beneath the sturdy walnut desk as a pair of smoke grenades crashed through the side windows, filling the room with a stinging gas.

"Close your eyes, Tyler. Hold tight to me." Oh, thank God, thank God. But Leland still had a gun. A lot of people still had guns.

"No!" Leland shouted in a rage. "Shoot me! Shoot me!"

"Drop your weapon, Asher!" That was Trent. His voice was muffled by the mask he wore, but there was no mistaking the deadly authority in his tone.

"Drop it!" Max was in the room, too.

"This one's dead," Olivia announced, moving away from Dr. Eisenbach's slumped body.

Jim Parker was there. Even Lieutenant Rafferty-Taylor had a bead on the man her team had finally brought down. "Drop it, Mr. Asher. You're surrounded. We have oxygen masks. You do not."

"No! You have to shoot me!"

Katie hugged her body around Tyler's as tightly as she could when she felt the barrel of Asher's recently fired gun singe the nape of her neck. "Don't hurt my son!"

Leland yanked on the collar of her blouse to pull her from beneath the desk. But six feet five inches of defensive tackle slammed into the older man and flattened him on the floor.

"It's over, Asher. You're done." She could hear him kicking Leland's gun away and pulling the handcuffs from his belt. "Sunshine, you all right?"

"Yes." The lieutenant helped her crawl out from under the desk and stand.

"Tyler?"

"I'm okay." Katie hugged her son tightly to her chest, assuring her boss with a nod as Max, Olivia and Jim circled around the imported rug where Trent was hand-cuffing a winded Leland Asher. "Mom, my eyes hurt."

"Keep them closed, sweetie. It's the cloud in the air. It's making Mr. Asher cry, too."

Lieutenant Rafferty-Taylor radioed backup that it was clear to enter and that they'd need two extra oxygen masks.

"Is Trent okay, too?" Tyler asked, hugging his arms tightly around her waist.

Trent Dixon, Katie Rinaldi's best friend, the man she loved—the man who didn't yet know how much she loved him—hauled Leland Asher to his feet and handed him off to Max and Jim. He peeled off his gas mask as the smoke in the air began to dissipate. "Read him his rights and arrest him for everything in the book."

Leland sneered at the much bigger man. "You're wasting your time, Detective. I told you I was dying. I was simply setting my affairs in order."

Trent leaned in. "You don't get to take the easy way out, Asher. You just confessed to two murders, and I bet we can close out a dozen more because of the evidence Katie sent us. More important, you threatened the lives of the two most important people in the world to me. Now, whether you have a year or a month or they find a cure for cancer and you live to a ripe old age, you are spending the rest of your days in prison."

Chapter Thirteen

The cold case squad and their loved ones filled up an entire row of the theater. Ginny Rafferty-Taylor and her husband, Brett, flanked the son and daughter who sat between them. Katie suspected they had a young starlet in the making with their daughter sitting on the edge of her seat for the entire show.

Uncle Dwight slipped his handkerchief behind Tyler's cousin Jack and poked Aunt Maddie, who wept silent tears at every poignant moment of the show.

Jim Parker and his very pregnant wife, Natalie, sat on the aisle so she could sneak out to use the restroom at several private intermissions. He wore a red tie and she had on a green maternity dress, adding a festive color to the group who'd all come to see Tyler in his debut role onstage.

Reporter Gabe Knight nodded sagely at several of the show's classic scenes, all the while holding hands with his fiancée. Olivia Watson might be a tough chick on the outside, but she was all smiles and thumbs-up to Katie as Tyler uttered the last line of the play.

Even Max Krolikowski, as gruff and Scrooge-ish as they came, draped his arm around the shoulders of his wife, Rosie. He nodded at something she whispered in his ear and pressed a kiss to her curly red hair.

They'd all been focused so long on closing KCPD's unsolvable crimes that it seemed odd to see this group of friends coming together to celebrate the holiday and show their support for a brave little boy who'd nailed every line and entrance, and whose very life was the best present a mother could ever have. Katie was grateful for her family and friends. They'd had each other's backs and saved each other's lives.

And when Tyler came out with the other children to take his bow, they all rose as one and joined the applause with the rest of the audience.

But it was in the quiet moments backstage, after the others had gone home and Katie was stuck in the green-room ironing costumes and ignoring Francis's blow-by-blow critique of their opening night performance, that she got the best present of all.

"Low clearance, buddy."

Trent ducked through the greenroom door, carrying Tyler on his broad shoulders with the same joy and love that Ebenezer Scrooge had carried Tiny Tim through the streets of London on Christmas Day. Trent even shook Francis's hand and congratulated him on his performance, rendering the temperamental actor speechless for a few moments before he beat a hasty escape.

"You ready to go, sunshine?" Trent set Tyler on his feet and hurried him into the dressing room to retrieve his coat. "I promised this hot young actor that I'd take him out for ice cream if he stayed in character for the whole show."

"And I did, Mom," Tyler bragged, galloping back out to join them. "I'm getting a root-beer float."

"Sounds a little chilly for a December night. Do you mind if I tag along with you for some hot chocolate?"

Trent leaned over the ironing board to steal a kiss. "Maybe it's me who should be asking if I can tag along and be part of the family celebration."

Katie cupped the side of his jaw in her hand when he would have pulled away. She lost her heart in the depths of those dark gray eyes. "You will always be a part of this family, Trent. You saved our lives. You made my son feel safe and you helped me learn to not just trust, but to embrace what I feel."

"And what do you feel, Katie Lee Rinaldi?"

"That I love you. That I've always loved you. I'm just sorry it took me so long to realize I'm *in* love with you, too."

Trent took her hand and led her around the ironing board to pull her into his arms and claim her mouth with a kiss. "I'm in love with you, too, sunshine."

Several seconds passed before Katie remembered they had an audience and pulled away—but only to welcome Tyler into the circle of this loving man's arms.

"Mom, you don't have to mail my letter to Santa. I already got what I wanted for Christmas."

Trent agreed. "I think we all did."

"I haven't said yes to your proposal yet." She felt glaring eyes from above and below and laughed. "Yes. Of course, the answer is yes."

* * * * *

Look for a thrilling new PRECINCT miniseries from Julie Miller kicking off in 2016. You'll find it wherever Harlequin Intrigue books and ebooks are sold!

Read on for a sneak preview of
LUCKY SHOT,
the third book in
THE MONTANA HAMILTONS
by New York Times *bestselling author*
B.J. Daniels

Max made a few calls to see what kind of interest there was in the photos of Senator Buckmaster Hamilton with his first wife, the back-from-the-dead Sarah Johnson Hamilton. There was always skepticism with something this big. But not one of the people he called told him to get lost.

"Where can you be reached?" they each asked in turn. "I'll have to get back to you... Is there any chance of getting an exclusive if these photographs...?" The questions came.

Not one to count his chickens before they hatched, Max still couldn't help feeling as if the money was already in his pocket. He could already taste the huge steak he planned to have as soon as he got Kat Hamilton to verify that the photos he'd taken were of her long-lost mother.

Then it was just a matter of waiting for the calls to start coming in and the bidding to begin. All he had to do was wait around until four for Kat.

He'd parked his pickup down the street, so he could watch the art gallery and see who came and went. A little after four, he spotted Kat Hamilton. She looked just as she had in her photo on her website. He watched her climb out of a newer model SUV, pull a large folder from the back and head across the street toward the gallery.

As he got out of his pickup, he admitted that he was

Lucky Shot

flying by the seat of his pants. He wasn't sure how he was going to play this. He just hoped that the Max Malone charm didn't let him down. Passing a shop window, he caught his reflection and stopped to brush back his too-long hair. He really needed a haircut, and a shave wouldn't hurt either, he thought as he rubbed a palm along his bristled jaw.

Well, too late for any of that. He straightened his shirt, sniffed to make sure he didn't reek—after all, he'd spent the night sleeping under the stars in the back of his truck. He smelled like the great outdoors, and from what he could tell, Kat Hamilton might appreciate that. Most of her photographs he'd seen were taken in the great outdoors.

Still, he knew this wasn't going to be easy. Kat Hamilton wasn't just a rich, probably spoiled artist. She was a rich, probably spoiled artist whose daddy was running for president and whose birth mother was possibly unstable. He had no idea what it was going to take to get what he wanted from the unapproachable Kat Hamilton.

When he pushed into the gallery, the bell over the door chimed softly and both women turned in his direction. The gallery owner looked happy to see him. Kat? Not so much. He saw her take in his attire from his Western shirt to his worn jeans and boots. He'd left his straw cowboy hat in the truck, but his camera bag was slung over one shoulder.

"This is the man I was just telling you about," the shop owner said.

Kat's gray eyes seemed to bore into him as he sauntered toward her. Mistrust and something colder made her gaze appear hard as granite. She was dressed in an oversize sweater and loose jeans, that approach-at-your-own-risk look welded on her face.

"Max Malone," he said, extending his hand. "I'm a huge fan of your work, but I'm sure you hear that all the time."

Her handshake was firm enough. Her steely gaze never warmed, just as it never left his. "Thank you." Her voice had an edge to it, a warning. *Tread carefully.*

"I was especially taken with your rain photo," he said, moving in that direction, hoping she would take the hint and follow.

"You should show him your latest ones you brought in today," the gallery owner said.

Kat didn't jump at that.

"Would you mind if I took a photo of this? I want to show it to my wife. This would be perfect for her office."

"That would be fine," Kat said, clearly not invested in his company. He was reminded that she came from a wealthy family. She didn't need to make money from her photographs.

He snapped the shot of her rain photo and then walked back to where he'd left her standing. Every line of her body language said she'd had enough of him. He felt as if he was chipping away at solid ice. Charm wasn't going to get what he wanted. He hoped he wouldn't be forced to buy one of her photographs. The prices were a little steep, and he doubted cash would warm her up.

He was tempted, though, to buy the one she'd taken of the pouring rain. There was something about the shot... "I hate to even show you the photo I took," he said, stopping next to her to show her a scenery shot he'd taken on his camera while he'd been waiting for her to show up at the gallery.

She gave the photo a cursory glance and started to turn away when he flipped to the one he believed to be of her mother.

Kat Hamilton froze. Her gaze leaped from the camera to him. She took a step back, her gray eyes sparking with anger.

"I'm sorry," he said innocently, even though he felt a surge of pleasure to see some emotion in her face. "Is something wrong?"

"Who are you?" she demanded. "You're one of those reporters who have been camped outside the ranch like vultures for weeks."

That pretty well covered it, while at the same time confirming what he already knew. The photo was of Sarah Hamilton.

"I guess I don't have to ask you if the woman in the photo is your mother," he said as he put his camera away.

"Do you want me to call the police?" the shop owner asked as she stood wringing her hands.

"No, this man is leaving," Kat said, glaring poison darts at him. She looked shaken. Clearly, he'd caught her flat-footed with the photo.

"For what it's worth, I really do like your photos." With that he left. She hurled insults after him. Not that he didn't deserve them.

He was just doing his job. He doubted Kat Hamilton had ever had a real job. But even though he could and would defend his to the death, he was always sorry when innocent people got hurt.

It was debatable how innocent Sarah Hamilton was at this point, though. Unfortunately, her daughters would pay the price for her notoriety.

MAX HAD PLANNED to drive back to Big Timber. But as he crossed Main Street, he realized that he was starving. His productiveness had left him ready to call it a day.

Stopping at a hotel with a restaurant on the lower level, he decided he'd stay in Bozeman for the night. He was about to leave his camera bag and laptop in his pickup, but changed his mind.

He knew he was being paranoid, but just the thought of someone breaking into his pickup, and stealing them and the photos on them, made him take the equipment with him. Earlier at Big Timber Java, he'd put the photos on a thumb drive and stuck it in his pocket. Still, he didn't want to take any chances.

He'd just sat down in the restaurant after getting a room, when the calls began coming in. He let them go to voice mail. He'd go through them in his room later. If he seemed too anxious it would make him look as if he didn't have the goods. He'd just ordered the restaurant's largest T-bone steak with the trimmings when he saw a pretty brunette sitting alone at a table perusing a menu.

She looked around as if a little lost. They made eye contact. She smiled, then put down her menu and got up to walk over to him. "I know this is going to sound forward…" She bit her lower lip as if screwing up her courage. "I hate eating alone and I've had this amazing day." She stopped. "I'm sorry. I'm sure you'd prefer—"

"Have a seat. I've had a pretty amazing day myself."

All her nervousness seemed to evaporate. "Thank you. I've never done anything like that before. I'm not sure what came over me," she said as she took a seat across from him. "It's just that I noticed you were alone and I'm alone…"

The woman looked to be a few years younger than his thirty-five years. After the day he'd had, he was glad to have company to celebrate with him.

"Max Malone," he said, holding out his hand.

"Tammy Jones." Seeing what was going on, the waitress set up cutlery at the table and took her order.

Tammy explained that she was a retail buyer for a local department store. She was in town visiting from Seattle. "I'm only in town tonight. I normally don't invite myself to a stranger's table. But I'm tired of eating alone and today I got a great raise. I feel as if I just won the lottery."

He told her he was on vacation and just passing through town. He'd found when he told anyone that he was a reporter, it made them clam up, too nervous that they might end up in one of his articles.

"I saw your camera bag. So what all do you shoot?" she asked, leaning toward him with interest.

"Mostly scenic photos," he said. "It's just a hobby." He didn't want to talk about his job. Not tonight. He didn't want to jinx it.

Their meals came, and they talked about movies, books, food they loved and hated. It was pleasant, so he didn't mind having an after-dinner drink with her at the bar. She had a sweet, innocent face, which was strange because she reminded him a little of Kat Hamilton, sans the gray eyes. He kept thinking of those fog-veiled eyes. Kat was a woman who kept secrets bottled up, he thought.

"Am I losing you?" Tammy Jones asked, touching his hand.

"No." He gave her his best smile.

"You seemed a million miles away for a minute there."

"Nope." Just at the gallery across the street where he'd seen a light on in the back. Was Kat Hamilton still over there? She'd brought in new photos, if that large flat portfolio she'd been carrying was any indication. He wished now that he'd asked to see them before he'd gotten thrown out.

"I know it's awful, but I'm not ready to call it a night."
She met his gaze with a shy one. "A drink in my room?"

How could he say no? They took the stairs to her room
on the second floor.

What could one more drink hurt? With a feeling of eu-
phoria as warm as summer sunshine, he reminded himself
of the photos he would be selling tomorrow.

When he woke the next morning, he was lying in the
alley behind the hotel. While he still had his wallet, his
camera and laptop were gone.

As HE STUMBLED through the stupor of whatever he'd been
drugged with, Max tried to figure out who'd set him up.
He knew why he'd been so stupid as to fall for it. He'd
wanted someone to celebrate with last night. As much as
he loved his job, he got lonely.

Now, though, he just wanted his camera and laptop
and the photos on them back. Maybe Tammy Jones—if
that had even been her real name—had just planned to
pawn them for money. But he suspected that wasn't the
case once he checked his wallet and found he had almost
a hundred in cash that she hadn't bothered with.

His head cleared a little more after a large coffee at
a drive-through. He put in a call to the department store
where Tammy Jones said she worked as a buyer, hoping
he was wrong. He was told no one by that name worked
for the company, not in Bozeman, not in Seattle.

He groaned as he disconnected. Whoever the woman
had been last night, she had only one agenda. She was
after the photos.

But how did she even know about them? He'd made a
lot of calls yesterday and quite a few people were aware
that he had the shots. All the people he'd called, though,

he'd worked with before and trusted them. That left... No way was that woman from the restaurant hired by the senator to steal the photos. If the future president had known about the photos he would have tried to buy them if not strong-arm him, Max was sure.

That left Kat Hamilton.

He drove back downtown. It was early enough that the gallery wasn't open yet, but the light was still on in the back. He parked on Main Street and walked down the alley. The rear entrance in the deserted alley had an old door and an even older lock. One little slip of his credit card, and he was inside, thankful for his misspent youth.

The first thing he saw was a sleeping bag in one corner of the back area with a battery-operated lamp next to it and a book lying facedown on the floor. The woman clearly didn't appreciate the spines of books.

He found Kat wearing a pair of oversize jeans and a different baggy sweater. Clearly, this must be the attire she preferred. But he thought about bottled up secrets. Was she hiding under all those clothes? She stood next to a counter in the framing room of the gallery, her back to him, lost in her work. "I want my camera and laptop back."

At the sound of his voice, she spun around, gray eyes wide as if startled but not necessarily surprised. If he'd had any doubt who'd set him up, he didn't any longer. She'd known she'd be seeing him again.

"I beg your pardon?" she asked haughtily.

He enunciated each word as he stepped toward her. "The woman you hired to steal my camera and laptop? Tell her I want them back along with the photos of your mother and—"

"I have no idea what you're talking about."

He laughed. "Did anyone ever mention that you're a terrible liar?"

She bristled and looked offended. "I don't lie. Nor do I like being accused of something I didn't do."

"Save it," he said before she could deny it again. "I show you a photograph of your mother, and hours later my camera and laptop are stolen and you have no idea what I'm talking about?"

Kat shrugged. "Maybe you should be more careful about who you hang out with." She turned her back to him as she resumed what she'd been doing. Or at least pretended to.

"Look. Someone is going to get a photo of your mother sooner or later. Why go to so much trouble?"

She turned to face him. "Exactly. If not you, then someone else will get her photo. Do you think I really care that you took a photo of my mother with plans to sell it to some sleazy rag? I didn't and I still don't. I've lived in a fishbowl my whole life. I've had people like you in my face with cameras since my father first ran for office. It comes with the territory. My mother is just another casualty."

He took off his hat and scratched the back of his neck as he considered whether or not she was lying. He'd been bluffing earlier. "I'm not buying it. I saw your expression when you recognized your mother in the photograph."

She sighed. "Think what you like."

"Let's talk about another woman, the one you set me up with last night."

Hand on one hip, she turned to study him openly for a moment. "What did this woman look like?"

He described her. "Don't pretend you don't know her."

"I know her *type*." She smiled, noticeably amused. "Come on, weren't you even a little suspicious when she hit on you? She did hit on you, right? That's what I thought, and you fell for it. Whoever set you up must know you."

Max laughed. Kat had lightened up, and he liked her sense of humor. "I'll have you know, women hit on me all the time."

She rolled her eyes. "Chalk this up as a learning experience and move on." She started to turn away again.

"You really don't think I'm going to let you get away with this, do you?"

She sighed and faced him once more. "What option do you have? Even if you had a shred of proof, it would be my word, the daughter of a senator, against your word, a…reporter."

Okay, now she was ticking him off. "I happen to like what I do, and it puts food on my table." He glanced at the photos she was working on. "Who keeps food on your table? I doubt your…hobby of taking pictures is your means of support." He cocked his head at her. "Then again, you don't need to stoop to having a real job, do you?"

KAT HAD KNOWN she would see Max Malone again after he'd ambushed her yesterday. He would want a story about her mother. He would use the photos he'd gotten to bargain with her. This wasn't her first rodeo.

But she hadn't expected him to come in the back way accusing her of stealing his camera and laptop with the photos of her mother. If she'd known how easy it would have been, she might have considered setting him up just for the fun of it, though.

No, she had expected him to come through the front door and make a scene once the gallery opened. She'd been prepared to threaten to call the police on him.

But he'd surprised her in more ways than one. Not

many men did that. So she'd let him have his say, waiting to see what his game was. She'd even found the man somewhat amusing at first, but now he was starting to irritate her.

"I'll have you know I take care of myself."

"Is that right? You pay for that fancy SUV you drive?" He laughed. "I didn't think so. Now about my camera—"

"If you think I'm going to replace your camera— What are you doing?" she demanded as he pulled out his cell phone and keyed in three numbers. She'd planned to *threaten* to call the police, but she wouldn't have done it because she didn't want the hassle or the publicity.

"Calling the cops."

"They'll arrest you for breaking into the gallery." She heard the 911 operator answer. He was calling her bluff. He knew she didn't want the police involved.

"I'd like to report—"

"Fine," she snapped.

He said, "Sorry, my mistake," into the phone and pocketed it again. He eyed her, waiting.

"But I don't have your camera or your laptop."

He studied her for a long moment. "Okay, if you want to play it that way, then what do you have to offer me?" he asked as he leaned against the counter where she'd been working.

She gritted her teeth. Hadn't she suspected that he hadn't really lost his camera or laptop and that he was playing her? She no longer found him amusing. It was time to call a halt to this.

"Even though I had nothing to do with the loss of your camera or laptop, I'll write you a check for new ones just to get rid of you."

He shook his head slowly, his gaze lingering on her long enough that she could feel heat color her cheeks.

He made her feel naked, as if he could see her the way no one else could. "*My* camera, *my* laptop, *my* photos. That's the only deal on the table, unless you have something more to offer."

"I just offered you money!"

He shook his head, his gaze warm on her.

She felt her cheeks flush as she realized what he was suggesting. "I have *nothing* more to offer you."

He raised a brow, shoved off the counter and closed the distance between them. "Either I get my camera back, or you're going to have to make it up to me in another way." He was close, too close, but it wasn't fear he evoked. She could smell the scent of freshly showered soap on him. Her gaze went from his blue eyes to his lips and the slight smirk there. The man was so cocky, so arrogant, so sure of the effect he was having on her.

As he brushed his fingertips over her cheek, she felt a tingle before she slapped his hand away. "If you think I'm going to sleep with you—"

"I said something that I would like *better*," he said.

Better than sleeping with her? "You really are a bastard."

He shook his head. "Untrue. Both my parents were married and to each other."

"You're enjoying this."

His smile belied his words. "It's purely business, I assure you. But I appreciate you considering sleeping with me."

She fought the urge to slap his handsome face. "I never—"

"I'm sure you have never," he said. "But we can deal with that later. Right now, I suggest we discuss this over breakfast. I'm starved." He moved away, finally giving her breathing room. "You're buying."

"I don't think so." She was trembling inside, her stomach doing slow somersaults. The man threw her off balance, and he knew it. That made it even worse. She took a couple of deep breaths, shocked that some reporter could get this kind of primitive response from her.

Finally she turned to face him. He was going through her photos with an apparent critical eye. She wanted to grab them from him. The last thing she needed was a critique from him about her art.

"Call the police." She crossed her arms over her chest. "If you think you can blackmail me—"

"These are good, really," he said, turning to look at her as if surprised. "You have a good eye."

She hated how pleased she was, but quickly mentally shook herself. What did he know about photography anyway? Just because he carried around a camera and took underhanded snapshots of people who didn't want their photos taken...

"I'd hoped we could discuss this over pancakes," he said as he stepped away from her photos. "I know something about your mother that you're going to want to hear before you see it in the media."

"There is nothing you can tell me that I would—"

"Your mother isn't just lying about the past twenty-two years. She's been lying since the get-go, and I can prove it." He smiled. "But first I want breakfast. I'm starved."

Don't miss LUCKY SHOT
by B.J. Daniels
available wherever HQN books and
ebooks are sold.

#1611 REUNION AT CARDWELL RANCH
Cardwell Cousins • by B.J. Daniels
The last of his clan to come home to Big Sky, Montana, Laramie Cardwell wasn't planning to spend the holidays chasing an elusive cat burglar. Now he'll move mountains to capture the mystery woman whose kiss smolders on his lips.

#1612 SMOKY MOUNTAIN SETUP
The Gates: Most Wanted • by Paula Graves
Wrongly accused of murder, FBI agent Cade Landry turns to his former partner—and lover—Olivia Sharp to help him find a killer...and a love that never died.

#1613 SPECIAL FORCES SAVIOR
Omega Sector: Critical Response • by Janie Crouch
To catch terrorists, agent Derek Waterman will need Dr. Molly Humphries, Omega's lead forensic scientist. Working together brings out feelings Derek would rather keep hidden, but when Molly's kidnapped, he will stop at nothing to save her.

#1614 ARRESTING DEVELOPMENTS
Marshland Justice • by Lena Diaz
When he is forced to crash-land his plane in the Everglades, billionaire and former navy pilot Dex Lassiter must partner with Amber Callahan to keep them both from becoming victims of a mysterious killer.

#1615 HUNTER MOON
Apache Protectors • by Jenna Kernan
Apache tracker Clay Cosen's past comes back to haunt him when his ex-love Isabelle Nosie asks him to help clear her name. Clay will need all his skill to ensure her safety—and win her heart.

#1616 TRUSTING A STRANGER • by Melinda Di Lorenzo
Wanted for murder, Graham Calloway has been in hiding for years, until he rescues a beautiful stranger, Keira Niles, from her wrecked car. For the first time he wants a future...but will the killer let him have one?

REQUEST YOUR FREE BOOKS!
2 FREE NOVELS PLUS 2 FREE GIFTS!

HARLEQUIN®

INTRIGUE

BREATHTAKING ROMANTIC SUSPENSE

YES! Please send me 2 FREE Harlequin® Intrigue novels and my 2 FREE gifts (gifts are worth about $10). After receiving them, if I don't wish to receive any more books, I can return the shipping statement marked "cancel." If I don't cancel, I will receive 6 brand-new novels every month and be billed just $4.74 per book in the U.S. or $5.49 per book in Canada. That's a savings of at least 12% off the cover price! It's quite a bargain! Shipping and handling is just 50¢ per book in the U.S. and 75¢ per book in Canada.* I understand that accepting the 2 free books and gifts places me under no obligation to buy anything. I can always return a shipment and cancel at any time. Even if I never buy another book, the two free books and gifts are mine to keep forever.

182/382 HDN GH3D

Name	(PLEASE PRINT)

Address	Apt. #

City	State/Prov.	Zip/Postal Code

Signature (if under 18, a parent or guardian must sign)

Mail to the **Reader Service:**
IN U.S.A.: P.O. Box 1867, Buffalo, NY 14240-1867
IN CANADA: P.O. Box 609, Fort Erie, Ontario L2A 5X3

**Are you a subscriber to Harlequin® Intrigue books
and want to receive the larger-print edition?
Call 1-800-873-8635 or visit www.ReaderService.com.**

* Terms and prices subject to change without notice. Prices do not include applicable taxes. Sales tax applicable in N.Y. Canadian residents will be charged applicable taxes. Offer not valid in Quebec. This offer is limited to one order per household. Not valid for current subscribers to Harlequin Intrigue books. All orders subject to credit approval. Credit or debit balances in a customer's account(s) may be offset by any other outstanding balance owed by or to the customer. Please allow 4 to 6 weeks for delivery. Offer available while quantities last.

Your Privacy—The Reader Service is committed to protecting your privacy. Our Privacy Policy is available online at www.ReaderService.com or upon request from the Reader Service.

We make a portion of our mailing list available to reputable third parties that offer products we believe may interest you. If you prefer that we not exchange your name with third parties, or if you wish to clarify or modify your communication preferences, please visit us at www.ReaderService.com/consumerschoice or write to us at Reader Service Preference Service, P.O. Box 9062, Buffalo, NY 14240-9062. Include your complete name and address.

HI15

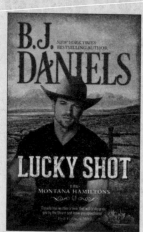

Laramie remembered hearing that an alleged cat burglar had been seen in Big Sky, but so far the thief hadn't gotten away with anything.

Until now.

Slamming on the brakes, he threw open the door of his rented SUV, leaped out and took off running. It crossed his mind that the robber might be armed and dangerous. But all he could think about was catching the thief.

The dark figure had reached the end of the roofline and now leaped down as agile as any cat he'd ever seen. The thief was dressed in all black, including a mask that hid his face. He was carrying what appeared to be a painting.

Laramie tackled the burglar, instantly recognizing his physical advantage. The burglar let out a breath as they hit the ground. The painting skidded across the snow.

Rolling over on top of the thief, Laramie held him down with his weight as he fumbled for his cell phone.

The slightly built burglar wriggled under him in the deep snow.

"Hold still," he ordered as he finally got his cell phone out and with freezing fingers began to call his cousin's husband, Marshal Hud Savage.

"You're crushing me."

At the burglar's distinctly female voice, Laramie froze. His gaze cut from the phone to the burglar's eyes—the only exposed part of her face other than her mouth. The eyes were a pale blue in the snowy starlight. "You're a...*woman*?"

In a breathless whisper, she said, "You just now noticed that? Could you let me breathe?"

Shocked, he shifted his weight to allow her to take breath into her lungs. This was the cat burglar?

He cut his eyes to her, suddenly worried that he had injured her when he'd taken her down. She motioned for him to lean closer. He bent down.

Her free hand cupped the back of his neck, pulling him down into a kiss before he could stop her. Suddenly her lips were on his, her mouth parting as if they were lovers.

The next thing he knew he was lying on his back in the snow looking up at the stars as the cat burglar took off. Her escape had been as much of a surprise as the kiss. He quickly sat up. He'd lost his cell phone and his Stetson. Both had fallen into the snow. He plucked them up as he lumbered to his feet. But by then she was already dropping over the side of the ridge.

Don't miss
REUNION AT CARDWELL RANCH *by B.J. Daniels,*
available January 2016 wherever
Harlequin® Intrigue books and ebooks are sold.

www.Harlequin.com

HIEXP1215R